Do No Harm

Do No Harm

AND OTHER STORIES

Clara Stites

Some stories appeared some years ago in the following:
"Zombie" in *Jabberwock Review*, Volume 24, 1
"Fish of a Feather" in *The Long Story*, No. 21
"Naming the Stones" in *Journal of Curriculum Theorizing, Volume 15*, Number 3, and later as a book by Spinner Publications, Inc of New Bedford, MA thanks in part to a grant from the Massachusetts Cultural Councils of New Bedford and Dartmouth
"Lines in the Sand" in *Paper Street*, Volume 1, Number 2
"Neighbors" in *Elixir* #3
"Reply in Blue" in *Furrow*, Volume 1, Issue 2
"Comfort Me With Lies" in *Puckerbrush Review*, xxiii, 1
"Green" in *Bellowing Ark*, Volume 20, Number 2
"Deersie" in *Timber Creek Review*, Volume 8, Number 2
"Do No Harm" in *The Larcom Review*, Volume 2, Issue 2
"Nesting on Empty" in *Other Voices* 41

Copyright © 2020 by Clara Stites
All rights reserved
Printed in the United States of America

ISBN 978-1-7351345-0-5 (paperback)
ISBN 978-1-7351345-1-2 (e-book)

Privately printed, 2020

Book design by Studio E Books, Santa Barbara, www.studio-e-books.com

This is a work of fiction. Characters, places, and events are the product of the author's imagination or are used fictitiously. Any resemblance to real people, companies, institutions, organizations, or incidents is entirely coincidental.

for
Elizabeth, Page & Gaga

Contents

Zombie	11
Fish of a Feather	23
Naming the Stones	47
Lines in the Sand	57
Neighbors	69
Gladly, Silently, Never	81
Reply in Blue	89
Comfort Me with Lies	99
Green	109
Deersie	121
Do No Harm	133
Nesting on Empty	143

Do No Harm

Zombie

WHEN I FIRST CAME HOME, my body was a wart, a mole, an excrescence. I did not love it. I did not see how anyone could love it. But if I attempted to say this out loud, my mother got grim and sad and silent and moved around the kitchen with her lips pressed together and her hands moving too fast and efficient as she unloaded the dishwasher or rinsed fresh berries for our breakfast.

It is blueberry season now; I came in time for strawberry season, and already we have almost had our fill of blueberries. I will go back soon; I've stayed too long, sheltering in the bedroom where I grew from child through girl to woman. I am almost ready.

I have been practicing love, learning my body again. Since June, I have come every evening to this old cemetery. NO ENTRY, DUSK TO DAWN. I park mother's blue Corolla on an unlit, narrow side street. NO OUTLET. I squeeze sideways between the stonewall of carefully fitted granite blocks and the rusty rattle of the chain-link gate. Each night, my mother watches me leave the house. I read the questions on her face, but she has learned. She lets me go. "Love heals," she says. "Time and love."

In the beginning, she tried to distract me. "Oh, Suze," she said on those first Friday nights, "I have such a craving for fish and chips, how 'bout the Bayside?" I went with her, pushed my fish around

II

the plate, drowned my fries in vinegar and salt, and talked about I-don't-remember. In spite of what my mother hopes, food cannot fill me or erase my body's betrayal.

At night before I go to bed, I stand naked in front of my mother's long bathroom mirror. It reflects these things: sink; tub; yellow daisies and blue forget-me-nots on the shower curtain; dark heap of clothing, mine, on the blue bath mat; tall, brown-haired woman, hollow-eyed and thin, her hipbones curving like the edges of a shallow bowl. The mirror cannot see the hollowness I feel. My mother cannot see it either, though she does battle with it daily.

"Surprise!" she said last week. "I told Maxine we'd take a kitten. For me. For company after you go." Maxine is my mother's best friend. My mother whispers to her on the phone, "She's like a Zombie! What am I supposed to do?" Now, because Maxine has promised that a kitten will be good for me, a bit of sharp-clawed marmalade fluff sleeps in my mother's bed at night and thunders through the house with sideways prancing, feints and leaps. If I sit in the big green armchair to read, the kitten curls into my lap. I find my fingers caressing her bright, soft stripes and thank Maxine.

Every Sunday, Steven calls from Kansas. "It's been so hot," he tells me, "terribly sticky and hot, the worst I've ever seen, you're lucky to be in New England." He is careful, he is gentle; he is losing patience. "It doesn't mean we can't try again," he says. "It doesn't mean anything's wrong with you."

"Yes," I tell him, "Yes, of course. Soon," I promise.

While Steven talks of weather, his and mine, I plan what I will take with me to the cemetery. Some nights I will go empty-handed. Some nights I will bring a blanket or bug spray or just the wine, white and cold. R. will walk in from the other side, the side nearest to his house. He will come with poetry in his head and his dog named Andrew Marvell on a leash beside him and always, always too much food: cookies, crackers, rich cheeses, smoked salmon, pickled herring, cashews, nectarines. R. believes in food and drink and, like my mother, in love and time and poetry.

My mother believes also in doctors. At her urging, I go once a month to her kindly, gray-haired gynecologist. He examines me and says I am "as good as gold." On my second visit, he gave me a printout, "Issues and Procedures in Women's Health: Partial Molar Pregnancy" by Francis D. Ashley, MD. The first paragraph contained words that hurt my eyes: *uncommon, very frightening, complication, hydatidiform mole.*

"I don't know much about this," my mother's doctor admitted. "It's just a freak of nature, something goes wrong. Two sperm, one egg, but instead of twins, you get an abnormal placenta and a fetus with too many chromosomes. Your baby never had a chance."

I could not read the pages he gave me. I folded them neatly, carried them away with me, and hid them far down in the back pocket of my empty suitcase. Perhaps Steven will want them when I go back.

"Help me with my garden," my mother said at the end of May. She handed me a trowel and a pair of garden gloves. I went with her to the backyard and knelt in the dirt while she broke up clods of soil and weeded the lettuce and tried to charm me with poetry:

"She digs in her garden

With a shovel and a spoon,"

Out of habit, I finished the stanza for her, and while I spoke she smiled as if a miracle were taking place.

"She weeds her lazy lettuce

by the light of the moon."

Then we heard the music. My mother rose eagerly, brushing dirt from her knees. "Suze, remember how you used to love parades?" And again I trailed behind her, this time to the front yard.

It is Memorial Day, and nothing has changed since I was

a child: the high school band; the firemen riding invincible on the new firetruck; the veterans with guns on their shoulders and triangles of extra cloth stitched into the backs of their pants, a record of how time has thickened them. "Go ahead," my mother says. "A walk will do you good," so I follow the music, thinking I will walk just a little way. Except, suddenly, deep purple lilacs bend toward me over a white fence. I pause, break off a few small branches, and carry them, still trailing the parade, through the open cemetery gates.

Ahead of me, the marchers turn to the right, raggedly in step, moving toward the flagpole in the center of the graveyard. I remember everything from years before: two Girl Scouts will lay a wreath; a Boy Scout will play taps falteringly and more sweetly than you can possibly imagine; I will brush tears from my eyes without knowing why they are there.

This year, instead of following, I veered off across the grass, looking for my grandmother's grave, a place to leave my lilacs. Grandmama is in the oldest part of this old cemetery, the part where narrow roads, designed for horse-drawn carriages and paved unevenly in cobblestones, lead past rows of broken gravestones. No one visits these graves. Because my mother lives nearby, I have daily walked or driven past this cemetery, and since Memorial Day, I have come here every night, but I seldom see another person except for the cemetery crew or R.

The crew consists of two men, old men who cannot match the pace of time. In slow motion, they mow the grass, trim the edges, rescue the broken gravestones and stand them upright against their bases. Day after day, forever, Virginia creeper, bittersweet and poison ivy edge over the fallen markers, and grass pushes up between the cobblestones like Sandburg's grass at Austerlitz and Waterloo.

"Shovel them under and let me work—I am the grass; I cover all."

— · —

Zombie

Late at night and in defiance of locked gates, vandals tip and smash the stones. I believe the vandals are boys from the high school down the hill, showing off, challenging each other to topple the tallest stones, and I am angry at their stupidity. My mother blames the city housing project and votes Republican because of it. R. insists that ghosts upend the stones. I tell him there's no such thing as ghosts.

"Oh, yes," R. says, "long-forgotten ghosts. I hear them calling out for plastic flowers, miniature American flags, visitors respectful in dark clothing."

That day in May when I first found my grandmother's grave, her stone was broken, split horizontally between the dates of her birth and death. Someone had leaned the top half crookedly upright in front of the bottom half. Only her name and birth date showed: SARAH GRINNELL, JANUARY 17, 1887. I tried to straighten the stone, but it was too heavy, rough and cold against my fingers. Today, I arranged my lilacs fragrant on the grass, wishing for a prayer that I could say, then turning toward the sound of guns—the veterans' annual salute to the dead.

While I stood startled by the guns, I saw a man behind me, watching from the shadow of a tree—middle-aged, an old brown dog beside him on a leash. The man was nondescript except for how he stared at me, and so I looked directly at him—never, ever act afraid—and saw then that he was not a stranger, but R. Years ago—ten, twelve, fifteen?—R. was my high school English teacher, the favorite of us all because so young, barely a dozen years older than we. The man walked closer and spoke to me with a question mark at the end, "Suzanne?" and I said, "Yes."

Just as R. can hear the dead demanding flowers for their graves, he saw my hollowness. He saw it at once, I knew. I felt his eyes on me, electric like the touch of a lover. I stooped to pat his dog. "You're back in town?" R. asked.

"Visiting my mother," I said, "and you? Do you still teach?"

"No, alas, and how I miss it."

"What part?" I am curious for the details of regret.

"So many things. Last night—and this is strange, I know—I dreamed the smell of chalk dust."

"So why have you quit?"

"My wife," R. said. "She has Parkinson's disease. I oversee her slow and daily disintegration."

"How terrible. I'm sorry."

"I don't like to leave her alone. This weekend, her sister's here. At night, home health comes for an hour or two. Otherwise, it is just her and me."

Next to my grandmother, another family, the Brownells, rests inside a scrolled, Victorian fence. The fence is iron and shaped to recall ocean waves. Even within the protecting fence, the stones have been broken and pushed to the ground, and someone has chiseled the rosebuds off the top of Nellie Brownell's marker.

That afternoon, the afternoon we met, R. and I went into the Brownell's plot and sat facing each other, the dog flopped between us, on the grass. R. imagined a patriarch, Lemuel, lying here with his mother—the roseless Nellie—his father, his sister, two wives, and the children, some stillborn, others "died young." Thirteen graves in all, a pair of Japanese dogwoods leaning above them.

The dogwoods were blooming the first time R. and I kissed here—it must have been mid-June—white petals spiraled down on us. This has become our place, this small and private garden next to Grandmama. It seems right to comfort each other among the dead.

Tonight is warm, late August. There's a soft small breeze and the moon is rising already, hot orange behind the copper beech trees whose roots go down among the bones. I enter the Brownells' plot and unpack what I have brought in my picnic basket. I spread a soft blue tablecloth on top of the only stone still upright, Lemuel Brownell's square monument. I let the edges of the cloth hang down to cover Lemuel's name. I arrange silverware, two linen napkins, two candles in glass cones. R. will bring our food and, tonight, our wine.

R. likes to eat, he likes to drink, and he likes to touch me, rub my back and arms, kiss me all over. We do not make love because we are married to people who need us. We have talked of this, turning it over like marbles in our hands, assessing our guilt or lack of it, deciding that the act itself would be betrayal. But often we lie naked on the mossy grass between the flattened graves of Lemuel's wives, wife one on our left, wife two on our right. And on most nights, when it is time to go, R. and I dress each other gently, straightening collars, brushing leaves and grass and withered petals of the dogwood tree from our clothes and hair. We walk to the gate. Always, before we say good night, R. holds me one more time. He is a man of ritual and cannot let me go without his poetry.

"But at my back I always hear
Time's winged chariot hurrying near."

R. is not in love with me, I know that and am glad, but he loves something about me: perhaps my breasts, my face, my sadness or the fact that we knew each other fifteen years earlier, happier then, innocent of death, nothing to each other except teacher and student.

He comes now from the far side of the cemetery, treading carefully between the toppled stones and uneven curbs. When I see R. from a distance like this, walking toward me through the dusk, his head full of poetry, I am always startled by his ordinariness. He is not fat, not thin, not tall, not short. He usually wears a red windbreaker, baggy blue jeans and grass-stained white jogging shoes. His hair has receded from his forehead leaving only a few thin wisps on top and a skirt of gray around the back. A small yellowing mustache fringes his mouth. He looks like a benign and bewildered hedgehog.

Tonight, he carries a brown grocery bag. His dog with the name of a poet pulls at the leash, eager to greet me. Andrew Marvell is R.'s excuse to leave the house. He ties Andrew Marvell to the Brownells' iron fence and lifts a bottle of Australian wine, a corkscrew, and two crystal glasses from his grocery bag. Andrew Marvell sniffs. "Cheese," R. says to him, then turns to me. "Wonderful cheese, and bread made just this afternoon." He kisses me sadly, opens the wine, fills our glasses, raises a toast to the dead.

"The grave's a fine and private place
But none, I think, do there embrace."

I step into his arms and smooth the wispy hairs that sprout from his bare pate. He pulls my hips against him, ready for the sex we will not consummate, proud of his desire. Over his shoulder I can see the bright lights from the high school field. There is music, the high school band practicing, preparing for the opening of school—I will be gone by then. A march comes intermittently to us on the dark wind.

"Be kind to your web-footed friends
For the duck may be somebody's mother."

I unbutton R.'s shirt so that I can feel the silky warmth of his skin. "How is she tonight?" I ask.

"Brittle and afraid. I said I'd be home early, but she won't know the difference."

Perhaps it is R.'s sadness that brings me night after night. "I've loved her thirty years," he says, "and she's vanishing before my eyes." Or perhaps what brings me is my own need to be held, to be loved. R. tells me I am beautiful. He knows how to touch me so that my body remembers it is a living thing. He says I have the breasts of a young girl.

"I am a young girl," I tease him.

"Oh yes," he says, embracing me. "I almost forgot. You are a beautiful youngish girl with breasts white and cold as the driven snow."

"You lie."

"No, it's true. Trust me."

"Sit down," I say, "let's watch the moon."

We sit together while the moon untangles itself from the beech trees and slides up the sky. The marching band finishes practice and disperses in noisy cars. R. and I drink the wine and eat the bread and cheese while Andrew Marvell stares hungrily at us. We will not come here again, we have agreed. Tonight is our last night.

In the front row of the Brownells' plot, three infants are buried side by side. Their grave is marked with a single long, low stone, its top carved into three small, connected arches. The stone tells us, barely legible, that these are the infant sons of Lemuel and Patience Brownell. Dead at birth; dead at three months and two days; dead at one year, two months, seventeen days.

My own child, my own dead baby, has no stone to mark his grave. What do they do with abnormalities after they scrape them out of a woman's body? I want my baby buried here between my grandmother's broken stone and the Brownell children. Grandmama will love him; the Brownell babies will be his friends forever. How would he look if his chromosomes had not been scrambled in those first three months? Dark eyes like his father to whom I will soon return? Curly hair like mine? A crooked smile that tilts across his face the way my mother's does? I would like to keep my baby company on nights like this.

One evening in June, when the days were long and the white horse chestnut trees were covered with torches of white blooms, R. and I walked Andrew Marvell along the cemetery's cobbled roads. If someone saw us, they thought nothing of it. A middle-aged man and his young wife, or perhaps she is his daughter, paying their respects. We read the stones aloud to each other

and imagined lives to fit the names. LAVINIA, WIFE OF CAP-
TAIN PETER HUSSEY, DIED AT SEA ON BOARD THE BARQUE
KADOSH, JANUARY 10, 1867, AGE 22. We looked for Captain
Peter's stone but could not find it. We were practicing with death,
learning its languages. Did Peter bring Lavinia's body home, we
wondered, or does her stone mark an empty grave?

R. loves the names of the dead. He keeps a list: Louisa, Bathsheba, Clarissa, Josiah, Charity, Peleg, Meriba, Silas, Lemuel. In June, I did not want to think about the stones, but R. read the names and imagined them alive. By July, I too could see the faces, watching them through R.'s eyes, then adding my own threads to their stories. Now, I dare to imagine evenings, father, mother, children at the kitchen table, reading, knitting, oblivious, the unsteady lamplight yellow and warm, the voices weaving round each other. That's all life is: a short time within the circle of a lamp.

At first, in June, R. and I walked and read the stones, recited poetry, wove stories for the dead. At first, that was enough; we were only helping each other with our sorrows. Later, we learned again how to touch, to kiss, to watch the stars, to tell secrets. This is how love goes, this is how it feels, here is what to say. There is nothing to fear. We can tell each other anything:

"I threw up, I nibbled Saltines, I was ridiculously happy."

"She can no longer smile; her face is frozen empty, she's trapped inside herself."

"I was so sure it was a boy, we had names, I thought that any day I'd feel him move."

"Our daughters don't visit, too sad, they say, to see her this way."

"A *wart* inside me, masquerading as a baby."

"Not a wart, not a mole, just a mistake of nature, no one's fault."

Tonight, there are cars on the street beyond the wall. We hear the thud of their radios. The engines are off, but the radios continue.

We see the shapes of people, nine or ten of them perhaps. Some sit on the cemetery wall, others lean against their dark, glinting cars. They drink, tipping back their heads to get every drop. They throw their empty bottles into the street. They laugh. Two girls stand and dance together to the music. They are thin and lithe; nothing bad has ever happened to their bodies. R. and I hold hands and walk farther into the cemetery, but the thumping bass trails after us.

We return to our fenced plot and the Brownells. We take off our clothes and lie side by side, caressing each other, soaking in the warmth of each other.

"What will you do?" he asks.

"I'm going home. I told Steven I will try."

"Are you glad?"

"Scared, I think. I said terrible things to him before I left."

I am still running my fingertips across R.'s shoulders and chest and face. "I'll miss you," I say.

"Yes," he answers for us both, and I begin to cry.

We hear voices and the sound of breaking glass. Andrew Marvel lifts his head and growls a warning. Off to our left, over near the beech trees, someone shouts. We hear a man's voice—only the sound, not the words—then cheers and laughter. The shadow people have left their cars and come into the cemetery. They are knocking down the gravestones, and I sit up, afraid.

The sounds seem closer. "Shh," R. whispers, "they won't see us here." I crouch behind Lemuel Brownell's gravestone and listen. I can feel the grass cool against my thighs.

Someone is running, steps swift and light, rushing along the cobblestones, then stumbling, falling. "Oh shit," a girl cries into the darkness.

"Are you okay?" another asks.

They are so close I hear their breath. I kneel naked behind the stone watching for motion, shadow, light. The girls are almost at my grandmother's grave. Behind me, I hear R. fumble with his pants, zipping them and reaching for his shirt. "Lie flat," he says, and tries to pull me down, his hands on my arms, but I push him away because I see the girls, two dark shapes at Brownells' gate.

"Oh look," says one, "a little garden," and I leap suddenly up and out from behind Lemuel's stone, naked and fearless. The girls see me, scream, snatch at each other's hands.

"I am a Zombie," I croon to them, walking forward, arms outstretched as if to touch them. "I am a naked Zombie, and I have come for you."

"Oh my god," one girl cries. She stumbles backward across cobblestones and grass. I moan at them like wind in bare trees. "Oh shit, oh my god." The girls are sobbing, laughing, turning, running full out away from me.

I stand motionless, and R. comes close behind me. Together we stare after the girls, listening to their flight. "A naked Zombie?" R. asks.

I fall back against him, laughing, twisting, trusting him to catch me one more time.

Fish of a Feather

ALICE DOES NOT DRIVE, has never learned, so every weekday morning she rides the bus to the village and walks the single block to the market where she works. One block, that's all, so the walking never bothers her, not even with the bad leg, except for the few days in winter when there is snow or ice. The bus, the walk, the job itself: these make up the texture of her life, a life with all its colors clean and dark, every stitch just so.

Even if you never spoke to Alice, just saw her at the bus stop, you'd think you knew everything about her. She is tall, her body broad and solid, its individual features—breast, hips, waist—settled comfortably one against the next. She seems a frugal, self-effacing woman who wastes no time on fad or fashion or embellishment. In summer, she wears plain-cut dresses of muted blues or greens and sensible black shoes with three-eyelet lacing. In winter, she adds a gray woolen coat, a knitted purple hat and sometimes boots, the kind you unfold from a plastic pouch and pull on over your shoes. In every season, she carries a black leather shoulder bag and a plain wooden cane with a no-skid tip of brown rubber. Yes, you'd say, here is a private, quiet woman, a woman who dresses to protect her anonymity. Except for the hat, that purple hat.

What are you to think of that small boldness?

You could set your watch by Alice—not on weekends, not on Christmas or New Year's, Easter or Memorial Day, Independence

Day or Labor Day—but any other day. Five mornings a week, she descends with care from the 8:15 bus, first the cane, then Alice herself. She walks past the village's post office and shops, crosses the little alleyway that leads to the boatyard docks, and vanishes into the cool, briny smell of the fish market.

Inside the market, Alice slowly climbs the creaking wooden stairs to her office. Sometimes Garth or Forrest greets her; sometimes she ascends to the second floor without a word spoken, and there begins the steady, soothing routine of the day.

Alice's office is a tiny closet of a space. Its plaster ceiling slopes so steeply that only a child could stand upright to look through the room's one window. The narrow window creates an angled view of gas station, parking lot and boatyard. Alice keeps her desk against the tallest wall, opposite the window and turned away from it so that she faces the wall. There, she has hung a calendar from a local insurance company, a bus schedule, and a picture of her three gray cats, Blinkie, Winkie and Nod. The plaster wall, no longer a discernible color, is finely crazed with a web of thin lines that speak to Alice of wind and the subtle shiftings of the building.

Alice takes the order pad from its drawer in the desk, sharpens two yellow pencils, pulls the phone a little closer. Twenty-five past eight, another day begun.

As bookkeeper, Alice keeps track of all the customer charge accounts. She sends out monthly bills and then reminder after reminder to the summer people. Money means so little to them, it seems, that they often neglect to settle up before returning to Connecticut or Philadelphia or New York, but Alice, to whom every penny counts, is patient and persistent. The rest of her job involves answering the phone and taking grocery orders—most often from elderly ladies and from women too busy with tennis or boating or perhaps children to do their own shopping. "Gifford's Market, good morning," Alice says, the clean point of her pencil poised above the order pad. "One pound of green beans, yes, if we have them.... And three nice swordfish steaks, oh yes, fresh this morning. Yes, I'll make a note for him to let himself into the house and put everything in the icebox." When the order is complete, Alice tears the page and its duplicate from her pad, attaches the original with a plastic clothespin to the wire Garth has rigged, and sends it downstairs through the pipe that descends from her office to the front counter. The copy goes into her files. Now and again, but certainly not often, the caller asks for one of the boys—Garth or Forrest, that means—and Alice stamps three times against the wooden floor so someone below picks up. A simple system, but it works just fine.

Downstairs, Garth and Forrest sell basic canned goods and vegetables—durable vegetables like cauliflower, turnips, squash and beets. They also sell Campbell's soups, loaves of bread, zinnias cut from a local garden, and fish. Fish of every kind, depending on the season. Fillets and steaks of cod, hake, halibut, sole, mackerel, bluefish, swordfish and tuna lie on beds of cracked ice in a long glass-fronted case presided over by Forrest, a man who has worked at the market even longer than Alice, and Alice herself has been there almost sixteen years.

Forrest wears gray striped overalls and a brown or yellow shirt with its sleeves scissored off for convenience just below the elbows; he is always lifting fish, cutting fish, reaching into lobster tanks or bins of half-melted ice. He is a solitary gnome of a man, short and hunched, yet so skillful with his fish knife that you can barely follow his motions as he cleans whatever you have selected from the case: sever head and tail with two quick blows; slice long and smooth through the belly; eviscerate the body. You want fillets? Steaks? Or will you stuff and bake it whole? If you are uncertain, Forrest is ready with advice, sometimes a recipe. "No frills, no parsley, no capers, but it tastes good. Nothing better than fresh fish cooked simple," he'll tell you.

—·—

Forrest lived alone in what had been his family's farmhouse on a country lane. He drove an old green panel truck that he had christened Bessie. Bessie did double duty as the market's delivery truck, and on its doors Forrest had stenciled a smiling fish and the store's name: GIFFORD'S MARKET—FRESH FISH AND PRODUCE SINCE 1920.

Although Forrest seemed to have no family or close friends, everyone in the village liked him. "A character, a real character," all agreed. "Good hearted, too. Remember how last winter he took in that old stray dog, that ugly shepherd mix? And now he won't listen to a bad word about her, just shrugs and says, 'She ain't much to look at but she's company.'"

When the dog entered Forrest's life, she was thin, ribs sticking out, coat mangy and rough, burrs in her tail, no collar or tags or any way to track where she was from. "Doesn't much matter, whoever had her didn't treat her right," Forrest said. "I think I'll name her Stranger, or maybe MissFit."

"MissFit is too cruel," Alice had warned, sensitive to the difficulties of being always on the outside of life, so Forrest went with "Stranger."

Forrest enjoyed the occasional glass of whiskey and kept a bottle behind the low, open-top tank where the lobsters crawled across each other's backs and swayed their pegged claws through the water. Once a year without fail, he carried his whiskey bottle and two paper cups upstairs to Alice's office. Alice wasn't much of a drinker, but a celebration was required because she and Forrest almost shared a birthday. Forrest's was early in July, Alice's June twenty-second, the summer solstice. Forrest was elusive or perhaps forgetful about his age, but everyone knew that Alice was fifty-two. Alice had been fifty-two for ten years, maybe more.

When Forrest came up the stairs, Alice always recognized his step and knew, from the sound of shoe against wood, the purpose of each visit. If he came to her office because something was wrong—the delivery truck wouldn't start, they were out of lobsters, old Mrs. B. had returned the tomatoes "all spotty and nasty, how dare you sell such inferior produce"—his step was different. Slow. Gray. Shuffling.

For the birthday celebration, he came quickly up the stairs, rapped his knuckles on the doorframe and entered immediately, no pause in which Alice could reply, "Come in." Barely glancing at her, he pulled the rickety extra chair away from the wall, slid it up next to her desk, sat, and displayed his offering of half-empty bottle and paper cups.

They had a ritual. "I can't drink in the afternoon," Alice said. "It makes me sleepy."

"Who will notice? Here, have a little. How can it hurt?"

"You know, Forrest, I never drink until the sun goes down. After that, a little bit of something helps me sleep."

"Important when you sleep alone. I know."

Except for Forrest, no one spoke this way to Alice. Knowing that, you might expect her to object, insulted by his words, but no, she only laughed. Forrest laughed with her, then opened the bottle and poured out two cups—one miserly, one generous. After so many years, Alice and Forrest had formed a united front against all that was new, all that was pretentious, all that replaced their wry humor with the efficient clatter of the cash register. Were they friends, you ask? Lovers, even? Friends, yes, but lovers never, no. Both so old, Forrest shrunken into himself, Alice carefully inconspicuous. Had either of them in recent years tenderly touched another human?

"Well, here's to us," Alice said, extending her drink toward Forrest's. She sipped and set her cup beside the green desk blotter. Forrest drank and refilled his cup.

"How's your dog?" she asked. "How's Stranger?"

"She's good," he said. "I was right to take her in. I like the company." He finished his drink, crumpled the cup and dropped it into the wastebasket beside the desk.

"I'm glad you didn't call her MissFit. That's a hurtful name. Stranger is kinder."

"I have you to thank."

"Yes. Well. You know."

The phone interrupted. "Gifford's Market." Alice took the order while Forrest listened, nodding, disagreeing, scornful, silent, amused and, when Alice hung up the phone, shaking his head and glancing heavenward. No speech necessary.

"Better go," Forrest said, standing and pushing the rickety chair back to its place against the wall. "The Cods are waiting."

"Just one minute." Alice opened the bottom drawer of her desk and from it lifted a package, carefully wrapped in bright tissue and silver ribbons, birthday card attached.

"Surprise." She handed him the package.

He read the card out loud. "Happy Birthday with Love from Your Friend Upstairs." He always read the card aloud; it was part of their yearly exchange. "Sounds as if you think you're Jesus Christ," he said.

"No. Just a friend," she answered, "and before you get a swelled head, just remember that I sign every card I ever send with 'love'. That's how my mother taught me. 'Why would you be sending a card if not with love?' is what she always said."

"Friends are good—upstairs, or even down." Forrest stood by the door, ready to go, yet pausing just a moment longer. "Happy birthday, Alice. Happy fifty-second."

Alice liked her job. She tucked herself away, secure in the sanctuary of her office. She did her work with quiet efficiency, took the day's orders with helpful courtesy, and let her imagination roam unimpeded through the lives behind those voices on the phone. In mid-afternoon—bills ready for the mail, orders delivered by Forrest and his truck, the truck named Bessie—Alice went home to her cats and her garden and her books. Yes, of course, paychecks could be bigger, customers less demanding, but why complain? Even the bad spots—a late delivery, a customer account too long unpaid, a dip in fish prices—all of these were more or less predictable and therefore manageable. Old Mr. Gifford, the third generation Gifford to own the business, stopped in once or twice a week, but he no longer felt more than sentimental interest in the market.

Gradually, he had turned over the day-to-day to Garth, the record keeping and check writing to Alice, and all the fish to Forrest.

But on a deceptively gentle day in early spring, a day devoted to raking leaves out of the backyard vegetable plot, Mr. Gifford had a heart attack. "Mild," he insisted from his bed in ICU, "no serious damage." To everyone's surprise, he was dead within two weeks. Customers brought flowers and condolences to the market and attended the graveside service where the minister spoke of fish—Jesus was a fisherman and through Him we have eternal life—and tradition and family. Mr. Gifford's two sons, one a landscaper and one a teacher at the high school, lived in town; surely they would carry on the family business.

With the burial taken care of, the Gifford boys let it be known that they had no desire, none whatsoever, to keep the market. They had wives and children and mortgages, they had their mother's nursing home bills. "No need to worry," they said. "You run the market, and we'll sell it as a going concern. Chances are, the buyer will keep everything like it is now."

Garth grimaced and said nothing. Alice put the whole thing out of her mind; the sale could take months, a year, who could say. Forrest cleaned fish and made deliveries and brought Stranger to work with him most days, no longer concerned that Mr. Gifford might object to a dog in the market.

"What's really strange," said Garth, looking slantwise at the dog, "is how quick she's getting fat." And yes, Stranger did seem to be plumping up. Forrest was proud, attributing her heft to his excellent care, but one day in May he went home after work and found six puppies in his kitchen and Stranger suddenly thin again, ribs jutting, teats hanging, a look of heartfelt apology on her long brown face.

What could he do but get Stranger's blanket from the truck, put it in a corner of the kitchen, spread newspapers on the floor. The next day he bought puppy food at Agway and a book on puppy care. "They don't do much," Forrest complained proudly. "Sleep, eat, mess. Sleep, eat, mess, but Stranger's a good mom, keeps them clean and fat."

Garth had three dogs of his own, and instructed Forrest in his canine duties. "You're gonna take her to the vet, right? Get shots for the puppies, get Stranger spayed quick before she does it again." Forrest grumbled a wordless response, cleaned another flounder, packed up two quarts of nice fresh steamers for Mrs. St. John.

Alice, because she wrote the weekly paychecks, worried. She had a vague understanding of Forrest's finances, or lack thereof. Cautiously, she raised the subject, disguising her concern for Forrest as scorn for the local vet. "Hate to think what that vet'll charge you."

"Don't you worry," Forrest said. "I'm going to sell those puppies, end up with a profit." He planned to take a photo of them, put it up so everyone who came to the market would see it. "Once you see that picture, there'll be no resisting."

When the puppies were ten weeks old, Forrest brought the photograph to the market. Six fuzzy, dark-coated little creatures with blunt noses and floppy ears peered out at the camera.

Behind them, Stranger stood watchful and thin. "I'm getting shut of them just in time," Forrest grumbled. "They're all over the house, chewing on everything—shoes, books, pens, the phone cord—it's like living with a gang of hairy locusts." He taped the picture of the puppies to the cash register and added a note that he had carefully printed out in square-cornered black letters.

PUPPIES!!
Healthy. Gentle. Playful.
Raised in family setting. Paper trained.

* * *

2 male, 4 female, $10 each, Available now.

* * *

Ask Forrest or call 6454

"That'll do it." Forrest stepped back to observe his work.

Garth came over, peered at the sign. "Have you named them yet?" he asked. "Maybe you should write their names on there, under the picture."

"No names. I don't want to start thinking of them as family. I'll leave the names for whoever buys them."

Alice came downstairs to admire the sign. Yes, of course, she would handle the phone calls, sure, no problem. But for two days, there were no calls about the puppies. Alice dealt with the usual mid-summer topics: Is it fresh? What's the price of lobster? Do you carry cocktail sauce? Breadcrumbs? Can you deliver this afternoon?

"I just need to get the word out," Forrest fretted. "I'll put a sign on Bessie's window, another out at Agway." Alice helped him make two more signs, but she remained apprehensive. She imagined Forrest sharing his house with seven dogs, Forrest driving Bessie while seven dogs crowded into the passenger seat, Forrest cleaning fish as seven dogs sprawled on the market floor alert to his every move.

Then on Thursday the phone rang. Nothing unusual, Thursdays were always busy. "Gifford's Market, good morning," Alice readied her pencil and order pad.

"Chief Davoll here. Tell Forrest he's got a fire at the house." The chief rang off, Alice stamped three times on the wooden floor, stamped hard, then stamped again, grabbed her cane and hurried toward the stairs.

She met Forrest coming through the office door. "Your house! There's a fire!" The phone rang again, shrill and insistent. Alice snatched it up, "Yes? Yes, he's here." She handed the receiver to Forrest, "Your neighbor."

Forrest listened only for a second before he said, "Jesus Christ, save the God damned dogs," and thrust the receiver back into Alice's hand. Alice heard his shoes pounding fast down the stairs. From her window, she peered out at the parking lot. Forrest was already at the truck where Garth was loading the afternoon's deliveries. Both men climbed into Bessie. Forrest jerked her into reverse, then into forward and out of the driveway. Alice watched from her window as they drove across the bridge and vanished from her narrow view. Then she went downstairs; fire or no, someone had to run the market.

Garth came back later that afternoon, riding to the village in a firetruck while Forrest stayed to watch the pumper wet down the last embers. Alice and three or four customers gathered to hear the news. When he and Forrest pulled up, Garth said, two pumpers were shooting plumes of water at the house. Garth told how Forrest parked Bessie and ran across the yard. How Chief Davoll called for him to stop, but he kept going until one of the firemen—Tony from up the road—grabbed his arm. How Tony held Forrest back until Garth reached them and took hold of Forrest's other arm. How Forrest wrenched out of their grip. "I've got a dog and six pups in there."

"I'll get them. Stay here." Tony whistled for backup, and he and someone else went in the kitchen door. "If anyone can get them, it's Tony," Forrest said again and again. Then Tony was back, running through the smoke. "Got two." He gave the puppies to

Forrest and ran again to the house. The other man came out, he had one more pup, but he shook his head at Tony.

Tony brought the puppy to Forrest and ordered everyone away, "Get back, back, away from the house."

Forrest's house wasn't big, Garth said, just an old two-story farmhouse, but when the roof caved in, the flames leapt high, roaring and snapping. Forrest sat on the grass and held the three puppies tight against his chest. Garth tried to lead him away, but he wouldn't move.

Later, on the ride back to the village, Tony had told Garth about finding the pups under the soapstone sink in the kitchen. Lucky he heard them. Howling like. Must have some hound in them the way they were howling. And yes, Stranger was there with the puppies, but already dead. Her body and the heavy stone sink must have shielded them. Tony was real sorry he couldn't save them all, real sorry.

When Alice got home that afternoon, she locked the front door behind her, turned on the hall light although the day outside was bright, hung her cane on the doorknob, peeled off her shoes and stockings, and called for her cats. Blinkie appeared, stretching and yawning from the kitchen, and slid his furry side against her legs. She picked him up and kissed the top of his gray head.

Alice loved her cats. So clean and quiet. Independent. You go your way, they go theirs. And when you need a little comforting, there they are.

Barefoot, Alice carried Blinkie through the house while she turned on more lights, a light in every room, even the rooms she had closed off years ago. The sun would be up hours more, but today Alice wanted to fill each room with light and know that darkness could not enter until she invited it. In her father's study, she lifted and examined, then dusted with a few puffs of her breath and set down again, the framed photographs of her mother and herself, her father and herself, the three of them and the family dog, the formal picture from her parents' wedding.

She seldom entered this room. This was the room—ground floor, next to the bathroom—where she had cared for her father during the two final years of his life. Sad years, Mama gone already, just the two of them, Papa and Alice, overseeing the disintegration of an old man. When Papa died, Alice had given away the hospital bed and the potty chair and recreated his study as exactly as her memory allowed.

Alice moved her index finger through the dust on Papa's desk, leaving a line that rose and fell like little waves. She must come in here soon and clean, get rid of the cobwebs on the lamp, shake out the long burgundy curtains and hang them on the clothesline, give them a bit of sun and air.

Her mother's sewing room was next to the study, on the pleasant southeast corner of the house. This room Alice used, often sitting in its bay window to read on a Saturday or Sunday morning. Tonight, she glanced around the room, turned on a table lamp, used her foot to smooth a wrinkle in the rug. Idly, she opened the old wicker basket filled with spools of thread and packets of sewing needles. In the basket was a faded Whitman's Sampler box where Mama had always kept loose buttons. "Look, Blinkie," Alice said to the cat who curled like a baby against her left shoulder. Alice shook the box gently to make the buttons rattle. "Hear that, Blinkie? Let's look inside, shall we?"

Just the act of lifting the cover of the button box took Alice back to the long afternoons when she was sick, confined to bed, everyone so frightened about polio. How she had loved to play with the button box, dividing buttons by color or by shape, counting them, stacking them, giving them names, asking Mama where this button was from, or this one. Mama had hovered around her, offering tea and soup, massaging Alice's aching legs, reading aloud hour after hour. Alice had been restless, angry, and frightened.

"What if I never walk again?" she demanded, and listened suspiciously to her mother's reassurances.

"It just takes time," Mama had said again and again. "Be a little patient. Learn to entertain yourself. Read, dream, sleep, grow strong again. Everything will be okay," she promised. "Really, it will."

Alice stirred her fingers through the buttons until she found her favorites, the two brightly painted red and yellow parrot heads. Long ago, she had given the parrots names and spent hours moving them across her sheets, pretending they could speak to her and to each other. She lifted one now and held it close to Blinkie's face, "Hi, Blinkie," she said in a small, high voice—a parrot voice—"it's me, your friend Scarlena." Silly, because Blinkie hadn't even been alive that hot summer.

Alice returned the parrot to the button box and carried Blinkie upstairs. She went into the two closed bedrooms, brushing dust from the dresser tops, smoothing the spreads on the unused beds, turning on a light in each room. In the third bedroom, the one she had inhabited for her entire life, she opened the window and pushed the curtains wide so the late afternoon breeze could move around her. Then she lay on the bed with Blinkie still in her arms and wondered how it would feel to have all of this, everything she had ever known or owned or cared about, gone from her forever.

If she fell asleep with Blinkie warm and purring on her chest, she could sweep worry from her mind like the cobwebs in Papa's study. But Blinkie was restless. He slid from her arms and mewed for his dinner. The other cats wandered into the bedroom and mewed along with him. "Pitiful, pitiful," Alice told them gently. "No food in weeks, I know. Down to skin and bones." She got up and went into the bathroom, washed her hands, combed her hair, followed the cats downstairs, and opened two cans—cat food for Blinkie, Winkie and Nod, and Campbell's vegetarian vegetable for herself. She ate her soup and a handful of Saltines in front of the television, but she could find no program to distract her from Forrest's losses or her own remembering.

Friday, Alice came to the market earlier than usual and found Forrest already there, pulling Thursday's groceries out of the back of his truck and sorting through them for fish or milk that might have spoiled in the August heat. Alice went to the truck and put her hand gently onto Forrest's arm. "Garth told us. I'm so sorry." Forrest smelled of smoke. A fine gray ash dusted his hair and skin like powdered sugar.

He freed his arm from her touch and gestured toward the truck. "Look there," he said.

Alice looked into the truck. On the passenger seat, she saw a wooden fish crate and inside it the three puppies curled together on Forrest's jacket. "Them and Bessie and the clothes on my back, that's pretty much everything left me."

As if the fire and the puppies yipping from their box in the back room and the usual Friday volume of business weren't confusion enough, Mr. Gifford's sons stopped in at noon. They'd found a buyer, a neurologist. He was opening a practice here. He and his wife were from Georgia, a nice young couple, enthusiastic about the market, want to keep everything the way it is. What good luck to find them. How fortunate to close the sale so quickly. The sons shook hands with everyone and thanked them for their loyalty to the Gifford family and admired but did not offer to adopt the three remaining puppies.

When the brothers had gone, Garth said, "Maybe it will fall through." After that, they were too busy with Friday customers, and then it was the weekend and time to go home. Alice had weekends off, but Forrest and Garth worked Saturdays. They were still at the market, piling ice over fish, when she walked to the bus stop. Too late, Alice wondered where Forrest would stay now that his house was gone. She started to turn back, just to ask him, just to make sure, but she saw his truck pull out of the driveway and cross the bridge.

When she reached the market on Monday, Alice saw that the side of the building along the parking lot had been painted with a long row of neat 3x3 foot squares of color. One square each of gray, green, yellow, brick red, and white marched across the market's weathered, unpainted shingles. Forrest and Garth stood near Forrest's truck, observing the squares.

Alice joined them. "What is it?" she asked.

"We're supposed to decide," Garth said. Forrest was silent.

"Decide what?" Alice wanted to know.

"On the color. We get to vote, she says."

"Who says?"

"The Wife. The doctor's wife. She intends to 'spruce things up.'" Garth shook his head sadly. "She was here all Saturday afternoon, painting those blotches." Forrest snorted and went into the market. Alice heard the scuffle of the puppies as they greeted him.

"He brought the puppies?" she asked.

"Nowhere else for them, is there?" Garth followed Forrest through the door.

Alice stepped close to the blocks of color and poked with her cane at each one. She didn't much care for any, though the yellow was the worst. She especially didn't care for such sudden and ill-considered change. What was wrong with plain old cedar shingles? Forrest came out leading the puppies on lengths of clothesline tied loosely around their necks. He lifted each of them onto the front seat of his truck, undid their leashes, cranked the window down about four inches, tossed in a handful of puppy kibble, and closed the door. "Stay," he said sternly as the three pups tumbled onto the truck's floor in search of food.

He turned to Alice. "If we have a hot spell, I'll have to ask you to keep them upstairs. It'll be too hot in the truck, and Garth says no dogs in the market. I think The Wife's got him spooked already. She's been talking sanitation and Board of Health." He gestured toward the blocks of color. "She's coming back today to see what we think."

"Oh dear God," Alice said and headed for the solitude of her office. On the way, she stepped into the little bathroom tucked under the stairway and poked at her hair. She should have worn a better dress, would have if she'd known The Wife was coming, but too late now. She washed her hands, dried them carefully with a paper towel, and started out of the room. But wait, how odd, she thought, to see a blue toothbrush—new, it must be new—a fat tube of Colgate and a razor arranged in a neat row across the top of the toilet tank. Alice lifted the toothbrush and examined its damp bristles. Forrest, she thought. Poor man, nowhere else to wash his face or brush his teeth. He'd better get this stuff out of sight before The Wife showed up.

The Wife arrived that afternoon. Alice stayed upstairs, checking her figures and filing slips of paper. She had decided to have no opinion about the squares of paint. She willed The Wife to stay downstairs, eliciting opinions from the boys. But no, there were footsteps on the stairs, then a tentative knock on the doorframe. "Come in," Alice said, turning in her chair to face the door. "I'm Alice, the bookkeeper." The woman in the doorway was small and thin and blonde and rather pale—perhaps all Southerners were pale. Alice had imagined Southern belles sipping mint juleps from frosted silver cups and wearing flowery hats and long dresses. This woman, The Wife, wore blue denim shorts and a t-shirt covered with tropical birds. Her shirt reminded Alice of the parrots in Mama's button box.

"It's so nice to meet you." The Wife came forward, her hand extended in greeting. Alice wasn't used to shaking hands, especially not with women, but she knew what was expected. The Wife turned to look around the office. She took a few steps to the window and peered out, came back to Alice. "What an adorable little room!" she said. "But don't you get lonely up here? And how do you manage the stairs?" she gestured toward Alice's cane. It was unusual for anyone to comment on her cane or her bad leg, and for a moment Alice was stunned by this intrusion. She hesitated, glancing at the cane. Before she had gathered her wits to speak, The Wife began apologizing. "I hope you don't mind, I didn't mean to pry. I do admire you so, the way you just go right on with life in spite of everything."

"I don't suppose there's much choice, is there," Alice said. She was careful to smile and to use her best telephone voice.

"Well, Alice, of course there's a choice. I truly, truly believe that we can find a solution to every problem if we just look long enough. In fact, my husband Harold and I—he's a doctor, a neurologist you know, so he understands these things—we've already talked about moving your office downstairs. There's that little room in back next to the delivery platform. There's nothing in there but an old couch and all those wooden boxes."

"Those are the fish boxes," Alice said. "Forrest likes to keep them; figures they're too good to throw away. They're useful for all kinds of things, you'd be surprised."

"I'm sure he's right, he knows simply everything, doesn't he, and I'll admit right off that I have *so* much to learn from all of you. But Harold and I hate to see you wasting energy on the stairs when there's a better option."

"I'm happy right here," Alice said firmly. "This is fine for me. And any color you want to paint the market, that's okay, too."

Within two weeks, the outside of the market was stained a canary yellow, its ancient shingles soaking up three coats of color and still retaining a stubborn streakiness. Things were changing inside the market, too. The Wife insisted the cement floor be painted the color of old bricks—"like Spanish tiles," she said. She hired a carpenter to add display shelves on the wall behind the counter. On the shelves she arranged framed antique drawings of fish, candleholders in the shape of anchors, soap disguised as starfish or scallop shells, and packets of blue and green and purple glass. "Scented beach glass," she exclaimed. "Isn't that fun?"

"Nine ninety-nine for beach glass," Forrest said to Alice. "She must think everyone around here is nuts." Yet they sold three packages of beach glass potpourri in the first week, and Alice had to add a new section to her accounting books: "Fish-related, non-produce." She didn't tell Forrest, but she liked the beach glass and the antique fish. In fact, she liked The Wife and found herself strangely moved by the woman's concern about the stairs. The Wife had asked several more times about fixing up an office downstairs instead of up. "We could make it very pretty," The Wife said. "You and I, we could make it so comfortable and cozy."

"No," Alice said, "absolutely not. You're very kind, but really I am happy where I am."

The Wife brought a pair of dimity curtains to hang in Alice's window and a picture of a country meadow to put above her desk. "Aren't these curtains pretty, Alice?" Yes, the curtains were pretty, Alice thought. White and clean, and they moved in the breeze if the window was open, but Alice tied them back with bits of string and hung the picture on the side wall. "Don't you like the picture?" asked The Wife.

"It's pretty. I do like it, but I like the plain wall too."

"But why? It's cracked, in need of paint."

She could care for this woman, Alice thought. May as well tell her the truth. "I like the wall plain like this because I see stories in the cracks," she revealed. "It's how I entertain myself."

"Like watching clouds? I do that sometime." The Wife touched the cracked plaster with her fingertips. "Aren't we silly," she said, suddenly a conspirator.

Tactfully, without a word to Alice, The Wife ordered a strong but unobtrusive handrail installed on the stairs. She brought in a plumber and electrician to redo the little bathroom: new toilet, sink vanity and mirror and, above the sink, a frosted glass light shaped like a scallop shell. That same week, she purchased three round metal tables and a dozen folding chairs and set them out on the sidewalk in front of the market.

"What's all that for?" Forrest asked when he saw the tables. Garth explained about the fresh brewed coffee and homemade muffins that people would buy and eat while they read the newspapers now offered for sale just inside the market door. "Gets pretty cold out here in winter," was all Forrest said.

Alice knew by now that Forrest and the three puppies were sleeping in that back room full of fish boxes. Garth knew too, but no one said a word. In the morning, before Alice went upstairs, she made certain to stop in the bathroom in case Forrest had left some telltale evidence of brushing teeth or shaving or washing up.

The presence of the puppies was harder to disguise. At first, Forrest kept them in his truck during the day, but this meant the puppies rode along when Bessie went out on deliveries. The Wife hadn't noticed, neither had the Board of Health, and Garth looked the other way. "It's his truck, what can I say?"

Then one afternoon Forrest stopped part way through making his deliveries. He wasn't out of the truck long, just long enough for a little conversation and bit of whiskey with a man he knew, but in that short time the puppies ate a loaf of bread and two containers of cream cheese crab dip—a new item recently introduced. "Everyone adores crab dip," The Wife had said. But the crab dip did not sit well with the puppies, who vomited all over the inside of Bessie.

Alice stayed late that day to help Forrest clean the truck. She carried out a bucket of soapy water, a roll of paper towels, and the tin trash can from her office. She watched while Forrest crawled around inside the truck. "God damned dogs," he said with pride. "Crab dip. Jesus Christ." Alice handed him more towels. The puppies scuffled together in the driveway, growling, crouching, leaping at each other, tumbling over in the dirt. Alice called them to her and stroked their heads. They panted and leaned their wiggling bodies against her knees.

When the truck was clean, Forrest gave Alice a ride home. "You must find a better place to stay," she said to him when he stopped Bessie in front of her house. "Sooner or later The Wife will find out what you're doing, and she'll be upset. Even if she doesn't find out, it'll be November soon and cold. There's no heat in that back room, you know." Forrest looked straight ahead as if Bessie were still moving, so Alice opened her door and got out. The puppies clambered into the front of the truck and reclaimed the passenger seat. Alice leaned in the window and smoothed their fur. "Did you have insurance on your house? Can't you use that for another place?"

"I had nothin'," he said. "All I've got's the land, five acres."

"Could you sell it? It's a pretty area."

"Maybe so, but I hate to break it into lots." He rubbed his face with both hands, then said, "I'm thinking I might find time to build something there. Small, nothing fancy, a little house for me, a pen for the dogs." Alice pushed the puppies away from Bessie's door.

"That sounds nice," she said.

From her front porch, she watched Bessie bounce down the street and turn in the direction of the fish market. Alice had a fenced yard and a garage. She could offer the use of them to Forrest, let him bring the puppies over every morning, leave them for the day. But what kind of a mess would three dogs make of her garden, and oh the poor cats. She stood on the porch for several minutes, looking down the empty street. Then she rapped her cane sharply against the top step and went inside.

The next day, Forrest tied the puppies to a tree behind the market. The puppies whined and flung themselves against their collars and tangled their leashes. Finally, the man from the boatyard threatened to call the SPCA. "Maybe that's the answer, Forrest," Garth said, "just get rid of them," but Forrest shook his head. He went into the walk-in cooler and carried out a huge bluefish that he slapped onto his cutting table and eviscerated with the skill of many years.

October was warm and golden and a time of harmony at the market. The Wife and Harold went out of town for three weeks,

Fish of a Feather

visiting family and friends back in Georgia. Forrest sold, or perhaps gave away, he wouldn't say, one of the puppies, the male. He took the two females to the vet and had them spayed, and early the next morning brought them back to the market, still quiet and drowsy from the anesthesia. He closed them into the back room and came to Alice's office. She saw he had a question on his mind.

"What is it, Forrest? Something I can do?" She could have stayed silent, sent him back downstairs, but she had gone ahead and offered, guessing already what he wanted. That day and for the rest of the week, the two puppies slept on a blanket in Alice's office beside the narrow window with its dimity curtains.

Forrest had decided to name them, and sought Alice's opinion. "Something catchy," he said. "Two words that fit together. Night and Day? Tea and Toast?"

"We can do better," Alice said. "Let me think."

"Bed and Breakfast? Fire and Ice? Hook, Line, and Sinker… except there's only two of them." Forrest looked at the checks—payments for September's charge accounts—stacked neatly on Alice's desk. "How about Credit and Debit? Or Null and Void?"

"Very funny, Forrest. How are you going to feel standing out in the parking lot shouting, 'Here Null, here Void'? You know what I think? I think one of them should be Stranger 2, in memory of their mother."

"That's nice. I like that. The other one I'll just call Smoky."

Forrest came upstairs each noon to take Stranger 2 and Smoky for a walk around the parking lot, and then returned them to Alice's office. Asleep, the puppies snored and twitched their feet, running in their dreams. Awake, they wrestled affectionately with each other, and squeaked the toy hedgehog Alice had brought them. When she answered the phone—"Gifford's Market"—they stopped their play and seemed to listen.

— · —

Three days ahead of schedule, The Wife came back, returning before Harold. Forrest—he was outside overseeing the late afternoon dog walk—put the puppies hastily into Bessie and entered quietly through the market's back door. The Wife called her three employees together near the cash register and talked about specialty food items, new shelves throughout the market, a wheeled wagon that could be moved outside in good weather to display flowers or local, farm fresh vegetables. And as for the back room, she said, that unloved little room would be her needlepoint studio. "I am just full to bursting with ideas."

Waving a rolled architect's plan, she urged Garth and Forrest and Alice toward the back room. "I'll get these wonderful fish boxes steam cleaned and use them to hold all my different yarns, and I'll put in a big window here, looking out over the harbor...." Garth and Forrest stood awkwardly inside the shadowy room, Alice behind them. They watched as The Wife saw and slowly understood the blanket and pillow mounded on the couch, the half-empty bag of puppy chow, the plastic dog dishes, Forrest's blue toothbrush, his street shoes, his extra pair of overalls. When she turned back toward the door, the eagerness and energy had drained from her face. "I can't believe my eyes," she said. "I don't want to believe my eyes. Tell me, please, that Forrest is not living here in this room? Forrest and those dogs."

No one spoke.

"Do you have any idea how betrayed this makes me feel?" Still no one spoke.

"And the Board of Health? What would they say about this? They could close us down, you know, if they wanted."

In the silence, she moved close to Forrest and stood before him, her arms crossed tight against her breast. "You must know, Forrest, that this is entirely unacceptable." She waited for his defense.

"I'm sorry," he began, "I just..." Behind him Alice leaned her cane against the doorframe. It slipped to one side and clattered onto the cement floor. The Wife turned, startled, toward the noise, but Alice paid it no heed. She simply stepped forward to stand behind and slightly to the right of Forrest. She settled both her hands firmly on his shoulders.

"Wait," she told him, interrupting whatever explanation he had been about to offer.

To The Wife she said, "I'm afraid you're jumping to conclusions. These are Forrest's things, yes, but he's not living here. Why would he, when he has a perfectly nice room at my house? Why would he want to live here?"

Garth looked quietly at Alice. Only if you knew him well could you have seen the smile incipient behind the stillness of his face. "That's right," he said to The Wife. "This stuff is all in transit. The blanket and the pillow, those are mine. Forrest is returning them; he doesn't need them now that he's at Alice's."

"And all the rest?" The Wife asked. "The dog food? The clothes?"

"That's all going home with me and Forrest this afternoon," Alice said. "In fact," she turned to Forrest, "this might be a good time for you to finish loading up Bessie. You know how my cats get when I'm late coming home."

"Oh gosh, the cats," Forrest said. "You never want to cross swords with a cat, that's for sure."

Alice turned to The Wife and with her fingertips touched the woman's delicate wrist. "It's okay. Everything will be okay," Alice promised. "Really, it will."

She took the cane that Forrest had retrieved and now held out to her. "Ready when you are," she said to him. "Meanwhile, I've got a few things still to do upstairs, so give me a whistle when it's time."

Naming the Stones

MY UNCLE ZOETH wanted help with the stones, and so I rode out to his farm in Dartmouth with the Cornells, who lived just a mile beyond him. The wind blew hard from the northeast that morning, spinning the last red leaves across the road. Cornells' horse spooked a little and tossed his head as we went up King Street, but he had settled into the traces by the time we climbed the long hill above the city. I sat on the straw in the wagon bed, and watched the harbor disappear, and then the road and the trees and the stonewalls slip by.

My uncle Zoeth was the last of nine children born to John and Carolyn Howland; my father was the first. The seven born between them had died in infancy, leaving the two brothers standing like parentheses, one looking forward, the other back. Uncle Zoeth taught me skills, practical ways in which to act upon the world. He showed me how to ride a horse, shoot a gun, snare and skin a rabbit, shingle a roof. My father taught me words, the names of trees and stones and sails and ships, and of the world he knew.

I was not born until 1849, and by then my father was nearly fifty. His hands were twisted by arthritis and his back and legs were bent by years of work. He had been one of New Bedford's master shipwrights, but I knew him as a man who walked with a cane and cupped his hand behind his ear when my mother or I spoke to him. Although he was no longer able to work on the ships, he went every day to the wharves at the bottom of the town. As soon as I was old enough to walk there and back, he took me with him.

Papa greeted everyone by name, the outfitters, the bakers, the coopers and the caulkers, the blacksmiths, carpenters, sailmakers and riggers, and all the men who made their living from the sea. When I was just four or five years old, his friends lifted me and carried me high on their shoulders. Now that I was older, twelve already, strong and tall, they called me "young sir," included me in their conversation, and offered me mugs of sweet tea. I knew the names of all the whale ships Papa had built or repaired, and I imagined him shaping the keels, bending the ribs, laying down the decks, his strong hands touching every board of oak or yellow pine or hackmatack, every fastener of iron, compound, or copper.

I think my father's greatest pleasure came from seeing the ships come home. If luck had been good, they returned from years at sea weighted with whalebone, baleen and oil, their crews eager to laugh and throw a friendly arm across Papa's shoulders. Papa and I could happily spend the length of a day watching the ships unloading their cargoes or being hove down for repairs and new copper sheathing keel to waterline.

When Papa's legs grew weaker, we rode to the wharves in his two-wheeled open chaise. My day would start in the stable, brushing and harnessing Daisy, our chestnut mare, and leading her from the stable to the front of our house. Papa would come slowly down the steps, pull himself up into the carriage and take the reins. On the days I did not have to go to school, I would ride beside him, eager to run his errands, deliver his messages, or listen while he talked about the ships and the bustle of commerce around us. From our chaise, Papa would point out to me the casks of oil, the busy docks and streets, the fine mansions on the crest of the hill, the busy rope works, Simpson Hart's sail loft,

Leonard's oil works. "New Bedford ships light the world," my father told me.

About the time I turned ten, the waterfront began to change. My father blamed the discovery of petroleum; my Uncle Zoeth blamed our fleet for overfishing the whale grounds. I never knew who was right, but I could see with my own eyes that times were bad. Ships returned, unloaded their casks of oil and their whalebone, and then lay idle, tied three or four deep beside the docks.

With the ships silent, the waterfront shops fell silent too. The riggers and caulkers, the coopers and the outfitters went without work, and the iron-staved casks of oil were stored on the wharves and covered with seaweed to protect them from the weather. "Waiting," Papa said, "for a better market that will surely come."

What came instead was war. More than twenty New Bedford whalers were burned at sea by Confederate cruisers, in April hundreds of men from New Bedford and neighboring towns volunteered to fight, and in May Lincoln ordered all the southern ports blockaded. When the blockades failed, the Navy sent out a call for ships that could carry stone south.

Suddenly there was a market for the whale ships. Papa and I watched ships return from voyages and unload, only to be sold immediately to a local company known as I.H. Bartlett & Sons. "What is Bartlett up to?" men asked Papa, but he had no ready answer.

Bartlett bought every ship offered and moved each one to the four docks he had rented just north of King Street. Sixteen New Bedford whale ships were berthed there now, nine more that hailed from farther down the coast. At Bartlett's docks, the ships were stripped, their tryworks dismantled, their ballast removed, all their gear piled together. There was work for all, striping and hauling gear, then constructing living space aboard each ship for officers and a skeleton crew. Nothing remained aboard the ships except sails and supplies enough for one short voyage.

As the work went on, days into weeks, Papa came home from the waterfront silent and sad. I could not understand his mood until I drove with him one morning to Bartlett's docks.

"Look," my father said. "Do you see what they are doing?" I shook my head.

"Look there, there above the light waterline, there in the counter," he said. And then I saw.

Into every hull, Bartlett's workmen had cut a two-inch auger hole. Into this hole a plug had been driven and bolted into place.

"Why, Papa? What do they intend?"

"I am told," he said, "that the bolts can be unscrewed from inside the ship. The plugs will be knocked out, the water will flow in. Have no doubt these ships are fitted for sinking."

I made no reply. I could only look about us at the masts of twenty-four ships and at the men swarming over the decks.

"They will load them with stone," Papa went on. "As much stone as each one can carry. Each to her registered tonnage, some more, some less depending on condition. There is a Mr. Duddy asking now for stones from all the farms."

And so, when Zoeth wanted help, I was glad to go. Glad to get away from the men talking to Papa in low voices, eyes down, collars up, hands pushed into the pockets of their dark coats. Glad to escape the workmen who were so busy on the docks and the young soldiers who marched off to war.

When the Cornells' wagon reached Zoeth's farm, my cousins Phoebe and Kate ran out calling my name and laughing at the bits of straw in my hair. The little girls were five and six, and their sister, Patience, had just turned fifteen. To my uncle's family, I was both son and brother, always welcome at their farm. Aunt Susan cooked special foods for me, cranberry muffins and the thick bacon she served up for breakfast; Phoebe and Kate hung on my arms, begging for stories or a game of kitty in the cradle; Patience teased me with her brown eyes and quick laughter; Zoeth called me "son" and relied on me to help with the heavy work.

But it was November now, and so the crops were in, the hay neatly ricked up in the fields, the potatoes and turnips and squash stored in the attic, the buildings snug with cornstalks and pumpkin vine heaped around their foundation. Yet even through the slow rhythms of the farm, I could feel the war. The Borden boys had signed up last week, the Cummings twins the week before, and more would follow, Zoeth told me.

The news had come back from Bull Run in mid-summer, the first sign that the war would be neither quick nor easy. "We ran," my uncle said. "We turned tail and ran like rabbits in front of Jackson's army. And now McClellan has them waiting, doing nothing, licking their wounds, while he makes up his mind which way to go."

Even when Zoeth sat in his own kitchen and talked to me about Fort Sumter, the blockades of Southern harbors, and the slaughter at Manassas, those places seemed too distant to be real. I couldn't think what it would be like to march away from home in a new uniform and new shoes and be gone for months or even years.

"Better get some sleep, son," Zoeth said. "You'll be doing your share and more in the morning." Whenever I was at the farm, I slept in the big kitchen, near the fireplace. At Zoeth's words, I spread out the blankets on the floor and made a pillow of my shirt and jacket and watched the flames against the rough granite of the fireplace. Tomorrow, I knew, I would work hard outside in the cold and the wind with its chill hint of the year's early snow.

I woke later to a scraping sound from the door and sat up quickly, but the light from the fire was very low. I heard the latch slipped up and the door pressed open, then shut. A dark, long-skirted figure moved across the room. "Patience," I said, but she knelt by my blankets, and the firelight showed her cheeks wet with tears. "Patience," I began again. She pressed cold fingers over my mouth, shaking her head. "Stephen Cornell goes tomorrow," she whispered. Then she rose and went. When I finally slept, I dreamed of the Cornells' boy marching away, part of a long blue line of boys without faces.

Zoeth had a heavy wagon that he used for moving stone and brick. Its bed was reinforced with rough-cut pine and set low between four high iron-rimmed wheels. I walked out to the field while Zoeth harnessed up his team of buckskins. Waiting by the barway, I could hear them through the clear dawn air, the creak and rattle of the empty wagon, the click of horseshoes and the rumble of iron rims across the stones on the road.

The rocks were spread everywhere in the rough field. "We had the cows in here," Zoeth said. "They cleared out the brush pretty good, but they left the stones." I glanced quickly at him, surprised at his wry joke. "We'll start with the big ones. Layer them out in the wagon bed, then build a second layer." The granite was cold, a hard flinty gray flecked with paler shades of feldspars and micas. I thought of the great glaciers rolling the stones down over the land, carrying them in ice, on water, sorting them by size and leaving them across the landscape.

Zoeth used the pry bar, lifting an edge of the rock so that I could get my hands under and around it. Then we would lift, roll, haul the rocks to the wagon, lift them up, lodge them securely against each other. The horses stood, breathing steam and stamping their feet in the cold.

"Horace Grinnell is taking down the wall round his pig pen," Zoeth offered. "I'd rather clear another bit of field. This will be all potatoes come summer."

At last we were done. "I think that's about all we dare carry," Zoeth said. The wheels of the full wagon sank into the half-frozen earth.

Zoeth cracked his whip from beside the buckskins while I

pulled at their bridles. The horses dug in their great haunches and pressed forward, and the wagon rolled up through the gate and onto the road. I scrambled up to the seat.

We started for New Bedford after lunch. Patience brought us out a basket of fresh bread and apples for the journey. Her eyes had dark circles under them, but we did not speak.

Uphill, the horses moved ponderously with their heavy load. Downhill they braced against it and snorted at the weight until Zoeth stopped to let down the drag shoe as a brake. The last leaves were on the oaks, hanging blood red and still, and the sun was sinking behind us so that our shadows were cast out ahead of us on the road.

When we got to town, Zoeth steered the wagon toward the waterfront. Near the docks, the equipment stripped from the boats lay in huge piles, awaiting auction. My uncle whistled between his teeth when he saw. "Your father," he said, "what does he say of this?"

"He doesn't talk. We don't come down here as often as we did."

"Perhaps he can't bear to see."

"I don't know."

A swarthy man in a blue hat waved us on down the pier. "Good men," he said. "Dump them 'longside here, we're not ready for them yet."

"Come on, son, we have to move each one again," Uncle Zoeth said, and we began. When we were done, our pile of rocks looked small in the darkness. Other farm wagons had come and gone, unloading near us, men talking quietly as they moved the stones. The ships were silent, dark, and riding high in the water.

We drove to Papa's house, unharnessed the buckskins, rubbed them down with handfuls of straw, and put them into the two straight stalls next to Daisy's box. My shoulders ached with the work I had done, and my hands were scraped harsh by the cold and the rocks. We went inside where my mother had a supper ready.

I sat with Zoeth and Papa by the fire and listened to them talk. Papa told Zoeth how Bartlett had leased the four wharves and purchased every vessel offered. "It was a mystery at first, and aroused much speculation." Their voices drifted around me. I tried to stay awake.

"They need 350 ton for every bark, more for the ships. It's a lot of stone, and where it's going no one seems to know. Seventy-five hundred tons in all, I'm told." That was Papa.

Then Zoeth, "Some say we're sending stones for the slaves to use as weapons."

"Perhaps. But there's a hole cut into every ship and fastened shut with bolts. And to be sure, every one carries two big augers."

Zoeth again. "Patience is taking it hard, the Cornell boy going today. And as for me, I don't know."

"There's the farm and the girls…"

"Yes, I have some thinking to do. I promise you, I will not act rashly."

"It's a sorry thing, tearing the country apart like this, so many lives…."

Papa shook me gently. "To bed, boy. You're asleep sitting up."

By the fifteenth of November, twenty-four ships of the Stone Fleet were ready to sail, their crews aboard, their holds packed with stone. For five days they waited at anchor in the lower harbor for the sealed order that would send them off. Papa stayed at home and told me nothing. Early on a Wednesday morning, the sailing orders were given. We were at breakfast when we heard the signal gun, and Papa sent me out to harness Daisy.

We drove out of the city along the wide new road that circled Clarke's Point and overlooked the harbor mouth. Even so early, the shore was crowded with people. A few had American flags already unfurled in the morning breeze. Papa drove until he could see the fleet clearly, and we watched from the chaise as the ships weighed anchor and shook out their sails. There was a band playing. Men and women and children cheered and waved handkerchiefs and flags. From the harbor mouth, the garrison at Fort Taber saluted with thirty-four guns. The fleet replied. I wished that Zoeth and his girls could be there, to see the proud way the ships went out.

Papa shook Daisy's reins, and we kept pace with the fleet as it moved down the harbor and around the point. I recognized the *Harvest* and pointed it out to Papa. He nodded, and together we began to name the others: *Maria Theresa…American* of Edgartown…*Rebecca Simms* of Fairhaven with Captain J.M. Willis in charge. "*Rebecca Simms*," my father repeated, "the best of the fleet; she's carrying 425 tons of stone, but wherever they're bound, she'll be first there."

I called out, "*Leonidas…Amazon…South America…Cossack… Garland,*" and again my father spoke. "Aye, the bark *Garland*, with that fool Commander Rodney French giving orders to all the rest."

"*Archer…*" I said, and Papa replied, "Carrying only 280 tons, she could take more if she were sound. *Courier…Frances Henrietta.* Bartlett almost missed that one."

"William Pope was bound he'd drive a bargain, but she brought about the same as all the rest."

"*Potomac.* She's old and rotten, patched all over with cement, but copper fastened." The ships were standing out into the bay, moving away from us under sail against the morning chop. The keeper at Dumpling Light fired off his signal gun. "A patriot," Papa said and named the last three ships. "*Herald…L.C. Richmond… Kensington.*"

The crowds were thinning out, going home. Those who remained stood silent. I turned to Papa with a question and saw tears on the old man's face. "That's it, then," he said "They won't be home again."

I thought of Zoeth clearing his new field for next year's potatoes and of Patience kneeling by my blankets. I thought of the blood red leaves of the oaks and the snorts of Zoeth's buckskins as they felt the weight of the stones. I thought of my father, shaping the wood beneath his hands, and I thought of all the boulders, lying underwater in a long stonewall at the mouth of some southern harbor.

Papa was looking out to sea and made no move to go. I reached across and took Daisy's reins from his hands. "Mother will be worried. We must go home," I told him. With a bright fire and a bowl of warm chowder, he would be all right again, I told myself.

Lines in the Sand

THREE LITTLE GIRLS spin in circles tap tap tapping the hard soles of their white sandals against the rusty brick red tiles of the floor. They wear wide-skirted diaphanous sundresses—green, yellow, pink, hair ribbons to match the dresses. Laughing, they collapse in a pastel heap on the rattan sofa and writhe there in delicious silliness. Nearer to the bar, the Sunday night fiddler crab races are finishing up. Mandy from the front desk holds the winning crab aloft while its sponsors cheer, and Stanley, the old dark-skinned cocktail piano player, strikes a riff of martial chords. Evening has slipped in, sharpening the startling blues and greens of the sea, skimming the bright flowering vines that crawl above the terrace, and glinting a long yellow light through the bottles ranged behind the bar.

Soon the children will be gone. Already their parents urge them toward the dining room, cajole them to speak more softly, stop their dancing, be nice to the younger brother who drags in their wake. Three families, I decide, traveling together, or perhaps they live here on St. Croix and are friends, connected through their children. The brother—he is four or five—pulls at the sash of his sister's dress, undoing the bow at her back. "Stop it, Daniel!" she whirls on him. "Mom, make Daniel stop!"

One of the women—blonde, emaciated, blue silk blouse, lime green pedal pushers—reaches for the boy's hand, but he ducks away from her and dives for another sash. The girls turn to face him in a defiant row. His father picks him up and, laughing, carries him into the dining room. The girls readjust their sashes and hair ribbons and follow.

The bar is mine again. A boozy sort of sanctuary where I can linger for the next two hours, three perhaps. I take my favorite table, two back from the bar, on the edge of the terrace, and order a glass of Sauvignon Blanc, expensive but good, and if I desecrate the wine with ice cubes I can spend the entire evening here sipping, diluting, watching the tourists—the couples and families who move noisily into the dining room. I will order from the bar menu and eat my Sunday supper in semi-shadow. I do not like the hurry and formality of the dining room. I am an outsider by choice, most comfortable alone, in conversation only with myself.

I have been alone all day. I spent the afternoon watching the war. I did not intend to do that, I was headed out for a walk along the golf course, but I switched the TV on, just to see, just to check, only for a moment. And I was ensnared, hypnotized by the images of war. The Navy planes smashing into the sky, the soldiers adjusting their gas masks. One of the soldiers, a girl, waves gaily to the camera. Baghdad Live is cast in eerie green while Wolf Blitzer talks and talks and, below the picture in tiny letters, crawls the news of the hour. I watched until the President came on, assuring me that God was on our side. Then I went to the pool and swam laps for forty minutes, working to exhaust myself, erase the images in my brain. What kind of God would countenance this arrogance?

The sky darkens. From the terrace bar, I see the distant lights of St. Thomas and St. John. Close offshore, the waves break on a reef and make a curling, breathing crest of white. The waiter, Anton, brings my wine and offers me the menu. He is younger than my son and insists on calling me Ma'am. "Thank you," I say, and

Lines in the Sand

watch him lope away between the tables. Twenty-five perhaps? Older? John is thirty-six, a Navy pilot, a husband, and a father. One daughter, the marvelous Marissa, age two and a half.

John is in the Reserves, but no, he reassures us all, he does not expect to be called up because of Iraq. And if his unit is called, he will not have to fly again. I hope he's right, but I cannot prevent the clutch of fear that snatches me when the TV shows planes taking off or landing on a carrier deck. I slide two ice cubes into the wine, toe off my sandals, and rest my bare feet on the ledge that runs knee high along the terrace. The wine is smooth, and the evening breeze touches my hair and wraps around my bare arms. I am surprised, even after three days here, that the air does not hurt my skin the way it does at home, back where winter still holds sway.

This evening, before I left my room, I tried to phone John. I had nothing much to say, but I wanted to hear his voice, or Bettina's, and be certain they were safe at home in Boston. Sometimes they put Marissa on. "Talk to Grammy," they instruct her. Marissa is a talker and loves the phone. I understand only some of what she says, but hearing her is joy enough. This evening there was no answer. I left a message about bougainvillea and the color of the sea.

At the piano, Stanley has begun a medley of show tunes. I like the sentimental drift of piano notes across the terrace and into the warm sky. Stanley sees me watching him and raises a hand in quick greeting, then slips into "As Time Goes By," the tune I requested two nights before. The sea shimmers and presses against the land as it has done forever, powerful, serene, oblivious to the affairs of man or the allegiances of God.

When I arrived on Friday, my nephew Perry met my plane at the little airport. I'd been worried. Would I recognize Perry? I hadn't seen him in how many years. But I knew him in an instant when he walked toward me through the airport. He could have been Russell, a gay version of Russell. Except of course Russell is dead, has been gone close to ten years. No more island-hopping for Russell and me.

Perry drove me cross island to the resort. As he drove, I studied his face. Russell's green eyes and straight brown hair, that little twist to the lips, the high cheekbones. Perry's hands lay on the steering wheel long and pale like flounder. As Perry drove, he pointed out historic sights and the buildings damaged years ago by Hurricane Hugo. "When was that?" I asked. I didn't care, but I wanted to keep the conversation going. I don't know Perry well enough to be quiet with him.

"1989. Terrible. Everything ruined and the island still not recovered."

"Your house?"

"Oh, part of the roof lifted off, and stuff inside blew away, but we were lucky. Compared to other people, I mean. Our neighbors lost everything. Look, over there," he gestured toward a low, ragged row of cement walls. "Those were houses until Hugo."

And so I told Perry about the fire, my fire. How it started in the apartment next to mine, how the firetrucks arrived, sirens shrieking in the night, waking me, warning me. And now, how fortunate that John will take care of everything while I am away. Insurance organized, furniture cleaned and deodorized, my possessions in storage until the new condominium is ready. I did not tell Perry about the smoke, the smell of it when I woke up. I did not tell him how viscerally I knew I could never live in that apartment again. John thinks that treating me to a week on St. Croix will free me from the fear. I am not so certain.

"Here we are," Perry said. He paused at the guardhouse and gave my name, then drove along a curving road lined with hibiscus

Lines in the Sand

trees. The Privateer is big, pink stucco, tile roof, gardens, pools, always a basket of polished apples and a bowl of rum punch available in the lobby. A welcoming sign by the punch bowl declares St. Croix the home of Cruzan rum.

I checked in and Perry escorted me to my room in one of the seaside cottages. We agreed, dinner together tomorrow, perhaps a trip to Buck Island Reef for snorkeling and a picnic on Sunday. "It's wonderful to see you," Perry said. "This will be fun. I'll call you in the morning." When he had gone, I shed my shoes and opened the curtains and the patio door. Wonderful. Flowers, sunshine, a tiny lizard leaping away, the sound of waves on the beach below. The ocean, still those exact shades of blue and green and spark that I remember but can never explain to anyone who has not seen.

I wanted to go to the beach, wanted to feel the salty Caribbean water against my legs. I rolled up the cuffs of my pants and went out, past the bougainvillea and the pretty swimming pool, onto the beach. The sand had been raked in careful lines. The pattern was marred now, late afternoon, by footprints and waves, but marks of the rake were visible still. A sense of order. Everything taken care of.

The water was choppy, piled against the shore by a busy afternoon breeze and clouded with sand and bits of reddish seaweed. I waded in anyway—up to my knees, that was my plan—but a few yards out I found the sand interrupted by a low coral ledge. A slippery ledge, rough on my feet, it shelved abruptly into deeper water. I tottered. A wave with a little curl of foam on its top slapped at my legs, then another.

I fell to one knee and put my hand down through the water to steady myself on the coral. The wave withdrew. My trousers were soaked, and the right arm of my blouse. Okay, I had wanted to get wet, and now I was.

I retreated from the sea, washed the sand from my feet at the poolside shower, and returned to my room. Unpacked. Rested a bit. Called John and Bettina to let them know all was well, paradise attained. Band-Aid for my knee. Just a scrape. Walked up the hill for cocktails and dinner in the bar. Early to bed. How quickly we can slip from fine to not fine, the dividing line so hard to see. Going into the water, I was young and full of life. Minutes later I was an old lady squatting in the surf.

I spent Saturday morning in the pool. The beach seemed less attractive than it did yesterday, and the scrapes on my hand and knee were bothering me—not pain so much as a reminder. In the afternoon, I rode the hotel van into Christiansted, eager to revisit the town where Russell and I spent so many careless hours. They were happy hours, I guess, though I have found lately that happiness, like safety, is hard to identify. The van left me off by the harborside fort. I wouldn't need a ride back, I told the driver, because my nephew was meeting me for an early dinner. "You could come to our house," Perry had said, "but Leo isn't feeling well so perhaps you and I should just go out."

I knew Perry and Leo were partners; they've lived together for years. But I didn't know about Leo's health. I was afraid to ask. How do you phrase questions like that? "Is it AIDS? Or just a spring cold?" Anyway, I was in pursuit of nostalgia. "How about that old hotel," I'd said, "the Commander, Comanche, something like that."

"The Comanche? Yeah, that's still there." Perry sounded hesitant.

"It was our favorite bar, Russell's and mine. How about we meet there for a drink?"

Perry agreed, though he sounded non-plussed. Once I got to Christiansted, I understood why. The harbor was there, the random assortment of boats, but the streets seemed narrow, dirty, hostile despite brave efforts to repaint buildings and hang flowers and flags from their balconies. I walked along the new boardwalk that rims the harbor. I passed open-air restaurants offering beer, loud music, populated by a few rough looking men. They glanced at me and turned back to their drinks. I passed shops selling Crucian knot bracelets in silver, in gold, in size tiny through huge, toe rings, earrings, navel rings, belt buckles. Anything you want, except I wanted nothing that could be bought and carried home. Those were tourist things.

I remembered a stone tower in front of the hotel, a tower surrounded by water. The hotel owner had kept his boat tied there, between tower and hotel. Honeymooners rented its round and airy suite. But yesterday when I found the tower, it was shuttered and decrepit. Its moat had been filled and blacktopped. Behind the tower was the old hotel. The Comanche. How familiar its low doorways, the balcony above, the vines and shadows, the smell of dampness and blossoms. Russell and I stayed here sometimes if living on the boat got to us, if we craved a real bed, a long, hot shower, a floor that did not move with the waves. And many evenings we came to the Comanche bar to sit with friends, other boat people, and talk and drink and listen to the beat of the island music.

Mostly though, we lived on the boat, wandering from island to island in a youthful daze of sun and sex, alcohol and marijuana. When we ran low on money, we advertised for charters. "Available for charter by the day or the week. Antique wooden yawl, lovingly restored. Skilled captain and crew. Leave your name and phone number with Milt at the Comanche."

We ran a fine ship. People chartered from us one year and then came back the next, wanting more. Russell sailed and entertained the guests with stories of boats and pirates and storms. I sailed and cooked. Russell and I, captain and mate. It was a good life, but not a forever life, we knew, and when John was born we sold the boat and returned home to New England.

I went up the stairs and into the Comanche bar, expecting everything unchanged. I looked for the huge fan-backed chairs—cobra thrones, Russell had called them—but they were gone. No, wait, there were two left, but how battered and shabby, the others replaced by white plastic chairs drawn up to scarred wooden tables. At one table two young women drank something blue and frosty from short-stemmed, bubble-shaped glasses. The only other person was the bartender, a woman my age, skin lined and tightened by years in the sun. I looked at her carefully, wondering if I might have known her when I was living on the island. I couldn't tell, and I didn't know how to ask.

"One?" she said. "Dinner?"

"I'm meeting someone. Just for a drink."

She led me to a small table near the bar, but I hesitated. "Could we sit over there, on the deck?"

"Whatever you want," she waved me toward the deck. "We have red wine, white wine, beer and anything with rum in it."

"Do you still have those good daiquiris?"

Then Perry was there, hurrying up the stairs. He was late. He apologized. Leo was very sick. They were flying to the States tomorrow. Leo had two children, and he wanted to see them. Leo thought he was about to die, maybe he was. God only knows. Leo's children have been urging him to come home, be in a real hospital, see real doctors.

Frankly, Perry confided, Leo has pulled this before, but what if he's right this time? What can Perry do but go with him? There's no way Leo can travel alone, not feeling the way he does. Will I be all right on my own? Perry is so sorry to abandon me like this.

I'll be fine, I told him. He had enough to worry about without me. But, I added, I hoped he had time for a drink.

Oh yes, in fact he needed a drink.

The bartender approached, greeted Perry, looked expectantly at me. I ordered a frozen daiquiri. "We don't have frozen, how about just a daiquiri?"

"Fine. Sure."

"They're the best on the island," she said. "Nothing but rum and fresh lime juice."

"The same," said Perry, "and maybe some crackers or something, I haven't had a thing all day."

I wanted to tell Perry about the bar, how it used to be. I wanted to talk about Russell, about living in the islands, about our boat. I told Perry a man named Dick Dale started the hotel. "A CIA man, Dick was, came down here on a boat and never left. He was a boatbuilder, I think, or maybe that was his son." I pointed at the sleek hull of a wooden kayak that hung from the rafters of the bar. "I bet he built that boat," but Perry was distracted, not hearing what I said.

He drank his daiquiri quickly and ordered another. "You?" he asked. I nodded. Why not. I hoped he remembered that he had offered to drive me back to my hotel.

"I can take a taxi to the Privateer," I offered. "Would that be easier for you?"

"No, no," he said. "I live at that end anyway. And it's not safe for you to be walking around here after dark, not alone. Maybe not even with me."

"Not safe?"

"Oh, you know. The usual problems," he said, waving worry away with an elegant hand.

So we finished our drinks and Perry drove me to the Privateer. I asked him to leave me at the main building, I asked him to let me know how Leo was doing, I told him again not to worry about me, I would be fine on my own. Once he had driven away, I reclaimed my table at the terrace bar. The bartender had installed a small TV, and he was watching the war. I couldn't hear the reporter, but I could see that American bombs were falling on the people of Baghdad. I drank more wine than I should, knowing that my head would ache tomorrow but needing the buzz to soothe me.

Tonight, Sunday, a pair of men come into the bar and take two of the four seats at the table next to mine. They wear Bermuda shorts, and short-sleeved sport shirts. Their faces are sharp and unlined, sleek like the faces of otters, and their hands are manicured. They order martinis, extra olives, ice on the side. Anton pauses at my table and takes my order for crab cakes with mango salsa and another wine. The men discuss their golf game. A birdie on the seventh hole. Anton brings the martinis. I open my book—I always carry a book—and begin to read. I want to discourage attempts at conversation, but it is clear that the men have no interest in me, a woman with gray hair, drinking alone at the terrace bar.

I am reading, but I hear Martini One say, "We have no choice, you know."

Martini Two shakes his head and rattles his ice. "But remember—there's no credible tie to 9/11. Doesn't that bother you?"

"Not at all. The man's a villain."

"But what gives us the right…"

He is interrupted by a petite brown-haired woman who comes up behind his chair and slips both arms around his shoulders. "Hi, guys," she says. "Did you think we weren't coming?"

Another woman, taller and bedecked with silver bracelets, laughs. "We wouldn't let you drink alone," she says as she slides into a chair and waves toward the waiter. I keep reading. This has nothing to do with me, yet I listen for every word. The conversation switches back to golf. Too hot this afternoon, they agree, but their Monday tee time is 8 A.M. Cooler then, more of a breeze, afterwards they'll go to Christiansted for a bit of shopping. The women order a strawberry daiquiri and a frozen margarita, no salt, please. Their dinner reservation is in ten minutes. Anton brings their drinks and mine. I hear the waiters in the dining room singing "Happy Birthday," then scattered applause.

Anton brings my crab cakes, "Here you go, Ma'am. Enjoy,"

Lines in the Sand

and the two Martinis order themselves another round. The bartender is switching channels on his little TV. First the war, live from Baghdad, then the Academy Awards, live from Los Angeles.

I am reading *Things Fall Apart* by Chinua Achebe. I am interested in his story of a strong man whose life is spun apart by fear and anger. I forget to listen to my neighbors until I am distracted by a flutter of little girls, the three dancers on their way to the ladies' room on the far side of the bar. They walk side by side, giggling, heads tipped together, voices quick with excitement. I glance up at them and smile, but they do not seem to see me.

And then, startling, unexpected, there is a scream from the rest-rooms.

I jerk around to look. The little girls freeze in their steps. The bartender stops mid-pour. Anton turns, his tray of glasses still on high. He glances back at the bartender then puts the tray down on a table and goes toward the bathroom. The bartender comes out from behind the bar and follows. I stand, uncertain, ready to help or perhaps flee. Another scream, Anton knocks on the door. LADIES it says.

Anton steps back, uncertain, then reaches out to knock again, but the door flies open to reveal one of the blonde mothers, the woman of the blue silk shirt, and with her the little boy, Daniel. The mother bursts out of the bathroom, pushing the child before her. "In there," she gasps, and Anton leans into the room, searching for the enemy. We—the martini men, the bartender, Stanley from his piano, the pastel girls, Daniel and I—huddle in the hall between barroom and bathroom. The mother points into the bathroom, directing Anton.

"Over there, on top of the sink. There, behind the vase," she cries. "There, oh look out, he could be poisonous. Oh my God, I think I'm going to faint."

Anton takes off his left shoe and slaps with it at something in the bathroom. The mother backs away, hands covering her face. "Got him," Anton announces, offering his victim to us in a twist of toilet paper. "Just a little old spider."

"I'm so sorry," the woman says. "I couldn't help it. I have this terror…"

"That's okay, Ma'am. He won't bother anyone now," says Anton and flips spider and paper into the toilet bowl.

Daniel watches from the hallway. I stand beside him. As the toilet flushes, Daniel takes my hand. He looks up at me and starts to explain. "Mommy's afraid. She's a silly mommy," he says, but his voice has a question in it, and I am pulled into his fear. How sweet he is.

"That's right," I reassure us both. "Everything's okay. There's nothing to be afraid of. We're all just acting silly."

Daniel nods and chews on his lower lip. His hand in mine is small and warm and slightly sticky. The blonde mother clings to Anton's arm for support. Anton looks at me and shrugs with his eyebrows while the pastel girls crowd into the bathroom, squealing at what might or might not be the blood of the spider.

Neighbors

WHENEVER KATE LEFT their long driveway—a quarter mile of dirt rutted, puddled and pressed in upon by poison ivy and bayberry—she watched for Joseph. He lived alone just down the paved road in the small, wood-shingled house where he and his wife had raised their family of three boys, or maybe it was four boys and a girl, or a girl and two boys. The children had grown and moved away, and the wife, whose name Kate never knew, had died last winter. "Fearful sudden," the clerk at the post office reported. "Standing at the sink, and *wham!* Just keeled over, flat as a mat and twice as dead."

    Now Joseph apparently filled his days by walking to the variety store two miles up the road, then walking home again. He moved slowly, with a fierce and childlike concentration upon the surface of the road, feet splayed out pigeon-toed and head tilted stiffly downward toward his left shoulder. He seemed to carry such a burden of pain that Kate often stopped to offer him a ride. Joseph would lean his head and shoulders into the car and talk and talk, snaking his thin lips across snagged brown teeth and coughing as if for emphasis into his curled fist. Couldn't drive, lost his license. Cataracts. Can't see a goddamn thing, barely find his own damned feet. Can't stay in that house alone. Too many memories.

Joseph had never accepted the offered rides, and eventually, because listening to his litany of sorrow discomforted her, Kate no longer stopped. Instead, she looked for him and waved brightly—sometimes he raised a listless hand to her, sometimes he did not—and then she would be past him, her neighborly obligation reduced to a brief image in the rearview mirror. With only the tiniest pang of guilt, she could continue on to post office, grocery store, dry cleaner, or library.

On Mondays and Fridays, she went to yoga at the health club. On Tuesdays and Thursdays, she spent the day at Children's Services, where she volunteered in the daycare center. She liked to be busy, she told her husband, to be involved in their community.

Today—it was a Wednesday in mid-February—she could have stayed at home. There was nothing she needed, no reason to go out except the silence of her house. Still, she had remembered a library book due back soon, and she might as well drop off those three shirts of Paul's at the laundry, and so she went. When she reached the end of their driveway, she found the paved road empty, dusted with a cold and blowing snow. No other cars, no school buses, no plows out yet.

She hoped that Joseph was still at home, cocooned in his silent house. Then something caught her eye. A dark, oblong bundle of rags lay beside the road, two or three feet into the underbrush. Had Joseph dropped his coat, she wondered, and then realized that the ragged bundle was Joseph. She pulled over and, leaving the engine and the heater on, crossed the road and pushed through the tangled greenbrier to him. He heard her and tried to sit up. Like an old dog, he leaned forward on his arms and swung his head slowly from side to side. Remembering his near blindness, she said, "It's Kate, Paul's wife. From down the lane."

"You're a good person," he said, and tipped sideways again onto the earth. Kate knelt on the snow-crusted leaves and reached for his arm. "Joseph, what happened?" she asked and knew the answer instantly from the smell of him. He radiated the odor of liquor and of something else, urine, she thought, mixed with that

Neighbors

peculiarly dusty smell of desiccation, loneliness and age. "Joseph, you must be freezing."

"Freezing," he repeated and smiled up at her.

"Let me help you," she said. "Take my hand, try to get up." She reached for him, not quite touching him, hoping her words would be enough. "Get on your hands and knees like you did before. Good, good, now up." He started to fall again, and she had no choice but to take hold of him. She had him almost standing, reeking, shivering, leaning against her, but when he tried to walk he caught one foot in a snare of briers and folded in upon himself.

"Can't."

"You have to."

"Can't." Joseph lay curled on the ground. The snow was coming faster now, hissing against the trees and the brambles and the fallen leaves. He wore no hat, no gloves, just a woolen jacket over a worn flannel shirt. Kate knew, just from that one moment when she had held him, the eerie lightness of his bones. "Joseph, I'm going for help." She unzipped her parka, pulled it off and spread it, still full of the warmth of her body, over him. The red parka was the only brightness in the woods.

"I'll be right back. I'll bring someone to help."

"No," he said. "No one can see."

"I'll be okay, I can see fine," Kate answered, misunderstanding his words until he said again, "No one can see. Don't let them see," and with sudden urgency pushed the parka away from him and scrabbled onto hands and knees. Kate gripped his arm, pulled him upright and then leaned into him, knowing that he could not stand unless she held him.

She must get him to the car. There, at least, he would be warm. She guided him, talking all the time as to a child. "Step, step again. There's a stone, don't trip. You're okay. Hold onto me, I won't let go."

At the edge of the road, leaves and briers yielded to snow-slicked pavement. Joseph started to collapse, but Kate was ready.

"Keep walking, Joseph." She was shivering, as much with fear as cold, and the briers had pulled a long snag in the sleeve of her cotton sweater. "If you stop now, I'm going for help," she threatened.

As if propelled by his old man's pride, Joseph shook off Kate's grip and stepped onto the road. Kate seized the back of his jacket with both hands to steady him. He must not fall. They walked like that, one behind the other, to where the car—it was her husband's car, a dark sedan—purred with warmth and safety. Kate had left the radio on, and when she opened the door, the sound of a Bach cantata spilled out. Joseph pulled away and shook his head. "I'm not fit," he said. Kate hesitated. She thought of his soaked and stinking pants against the black leather of the seat and the way his smell would permeate Paul's car. Joseph seemed to read her mind.

"Your husband doesn't like me," he said. Then he grinned, dipping his head toward the ground as if suddenly shy. "But then, I've never cared much for your husband."

Kate closed the passenger door and opened the one behind it. Maybe he would be more comfortable in the back. Maybe he would want to lie down across the seat. She grasped his arm and steered him into the car, holding her other hand above his head so he wouldn't bump against the door frame.

Even with Joseph in the back seat, his stench surrounded her the moment she slid behind the wheel. She lowered her window halfway, turned off the radio and clicked the heat to HIGH. "Where shall I take you, Joseph?"

He said nothing.

"Shall I take you to your house?" Again, nothing. Kate turned to look at him. His eyes were closed. "Joseph?" she asked, but he seemed to be asleep. His head lolled against the window, and his lips quivered slightly as he breathed. Kate watched, wondering what to do. The skin of Joseph's hands was cracked and red. She saw that he had cut his right hand, caught it in the briers probably. A thin line of blood smeared his skin, but the blood was dry already, or frozen perhaps. How long had he been out here, lying in the snow?

She could take him back to his house, but then what? She should not leave him there alone. And he had made it clear that no one was to know of his disgrace. Kate thought of the clerk at the post office, imagined him describing Joseph with casual cruelty as he handed out the mail. Keeled over. Drunk as a skunk. Pissed his pants.

Kate put the car into reverse. She backed past their driveway, braked, shifted into drive and retraced the single set of tire tracks she had made on her way out. Paul was in Chicago, would not return for two more days. She could get Joseph inside, build up the fire in the woodstove, and let him rest until he was ready to go home. There was coffee already brewed, though cold now, and bagels in the freezer, she was sure. Or she could scramble up some eggs. He probably needed protein, and it would be nice for him to spend a little time in her clean, warm house.

She parked as close as possible to the back door of the house and turned off the engine.

When she glanced at Joseph in her rearview mirror, she saw that he was awake. "Your house," he said, with a question in his voice.

"Yes," she said. "I want you to come in and get warm, eat something maybe. After that, I'll take you home, okay?"

Joseph nodded. "Big house," he said. "Nice and big." Kate got out of the car, walked around it and opened the door for him. He swung his legs out and stamped his feet tentatively on the frozen ground. His eyes moved over the house, pausing at the complicated roofline and the Palladian window that let such lovely light into the stairwell. "How long you live here?"

"Five years, a little more, I guess. We built the house ourselves. Not the actual construction, of course, but the design, the way it blends with the landscape. Paul's an architect, and he says this is his dream house. Our dream house."

"Big house." Joseph said again. "Very fancy."

"It's big for just two people, I know, but we wanted plenty of room for guests. And maybe a child someday."

"Big. Lonely too, I bet."

Kate remembered the parka she'd left lying in the woods. She wanted it, the warmth and weight of it, and she wanted also a house that was smaller, older, more worn down with family and living. But how silly, ungrateful almost, for her to feel apologetic because she and Paul had a nice life. "Come on," she said and touched the old man's arm. "It's warm inside."

Joseph shuffled up the three low steps, followed Kate across the redwood deck and stepped in through the back door that she held wide for him. He was walking more steadily now and looking around with interest. How long did it take someone his age to sober up? Not long, she hoped. She led Joseph into the living room. "Water view," he said. "Very fancy." She left him there, gazing out the window as if something puzzled him.

She could put that old Polar fleece blanket over one of the chairs, telling Joseph it was for warmth but knowing also that it would protect the chair. She was gone only for a moment, just to the linen closet and back. When she returned with the blanket, Joseph had slumped into the big white armchair near the window. "Oh," she said, "that's my husband's favorite chair." But Joseph was asleep.

She watched him, pitying his loneliness and the gray, worn texture of his skin. Paul would tell her she was a fool to bring this man into their home. "What were you thinking," he would ask, "playing Lady Bountiful to the poor benighted neighbors?" But even Paul would stop—surely he would stop—to help an old man who'd fallen in the snow.

Kate unfolded the blanket and covered Joseph gently with it. Let him sleep, poor thing, the poor old man. Then she went to Paul's closet in search of clothes to lend him. Paul's suits hung straight and clean, good dark suits, expensive and well cared for. Paul's shoes were polished and paired on their own shelf. Paul's dress shirts, lightly starched and still in the laundry's plastic sleeves, were arranged by color on another shelf. White, blue, yellow, subtle stripes.

There was nothing there to offer Joseph, but in a lower drawer Kate found the clothes Paul wore when he was home. "My country gentleman clothes," he called them. She chose a faded chamois shirt and corduroy trousers. Paul's ample clothes would hang on Joseph's narrow frame, but they would be dry, at least, and clean. She carried the clothes into the living room and set them silently on the ottoman beside the chair where Joseph slept. Paul might well protest her easy charity, but he would never know. By the time he got home, the clothes would be back in the drawer, smelling only of laundry soap and the light fragrance that clung to everything in his closet.

Joseph slept for half an hour, snoring raggedly and once crying out a word that Kate, listening for him as she idly unloaded the dishwasher, could not decipher. When he woke, he was suddenly talkative. He knew this place, he told her. Used to hunt here. Hunted with his boys, but they're gone now. Moved off. Never visit, never call.

As he talked, he surveyed the room and squinted out the window. Then he turned toward Kate. "Of course all that was long ago, before your time, back when there was nothing here but beach plum and salt marsh, a few cedars. Before you put up this big house."

"We love the house. It's such a special place," Kate said, what she and Paul always said, but today the words sounded as meaningless as moths against a window screen. Joseph regarded her thoughtfully.

"You mind if I take my boots off?" Joseph gestured toward the ottoman. "I'd hate to put these dirty boots on that fancy bench."

He bent forward, and Kate saw that he had already undone the laces. He pulled the boots off and let them drop beside the chair. Then he peeled off his thin white socks, rolled them together, and stuffed them into one of the boots.

"How about some coffee, Joseph? Or maybe tea, or soup. Maybe some nice warm soup?"

"Coffee, if you've got milk. I always put milk in, didn't used to, used to take my coffee black, but now I find the milk stops it from riling up my stomach."

When Kate returned with a china mug of murky coffee, Joseph had left the chair and was running his hands lightly along the window frames. He turned to her. "I always wondered about this house. I'm a carpenter, maybe you know, or was before my eyes went bad. Now I can't tell good work for certain till I touch the wood, see how the corners fit together. Nice house. Very fancy."

"Paul and I feel so lucky to live here."

"Lucky, yes. And not hurting for money." Joseph sank into the chair again and stretched his knobby, blue-veined feet across the ottoman in a gesture so intimate that Kate turned sharply away from him. "I've seen the husband and you, the two of you sitting here, warm and cozy, reading books. I've thought a couple of times of paying you a call, a social call. Neighborly, you know."

"Well, certainly. You could have. You're always welcome." As Kate spoke, thoughts flicked through her mind like rabbits in a field. Where had Joseph stood as he watched them turn the pages of their books? How close had he come to their lighted windows? She and Paul never pulled the shades at night, didn't even have curtains in the living room.

When Kate turned back to Joseph, he was watching her carefully. "Like I told you, I can't see a damned thing anymore. Different shapes, light and dark, that's about it. Don't you start worrying about old Joseph looking in on you. Poor old Joseph wouldn't hurt a flea. Poor old Joseph wouldn't even see a flea unless it bit him."

"Of course not, of course you wouldn't." Kate backed toward the kitchen. When Joseph rose to follow her, she held up a hand to stop him, but he moved closer.

"I can't see you too good either," he said, "but I can tell that you're a sad one. You and old Joseph, we're quite a pair." He reached forward, tentative, apologetic, hungry for her embrace. Kate remembered the snow and the briers and the lightness of the old man's bones. All he wanted was a hug, a simple hug. How long—weeks, months, a year or more—since someone held him? But then he was so close, almost touching her, and talking, still talking. "Lonely old coot like me, sad little lady like you. Quite a pair." His cloudy eyes and curled brown mouth swam toward her.

"No," Kate recoiled, stepping back, away from him, frightened by his moist closeness, yes, and by her own stabbing need of comfort. She gestured angrily toward the ottoman so that Joseph lowered his arms—slowly let them sink—and looked where she was pointing. "Joseph," she said, "there are some clothes. They're dry, they're clean. I want you to put them on, and then you need to go home." She went to the ottoman, lifted the clothes and pushed them toward him. "Take them, please."

"Your husband's clothes," Joseph said, touching the chamois shirt. "I don't need your husband's clothes." He lifted the shirt from Kate's arms, shook it out and looked closely at it. "I never much liked your husband, did I tell you that?"

"You told me."

"I hope he treats you right, I hope he does. But there's something makes you sad, and if I had to guess, I'd say it's him. Or maybe it's living out here, me your only neighbor, no children, not even a dog or a cat. Makes a person wonder, you know."

"Paul's allergic to animals, we can't have any pets."

"Allergic. He allergic to children too? They make him sneeze, maybe?"

"That's none of your business, Joseph. You don't know a thing about us, not one thing."

"I know lonely."

"You don't know me, Joseph."

"There's things I see, blind or not. Like my father used to say, 'There's a weasel in the woodpile.'"

Kate dropped her armful of clothing and took the shirt from Joseph's hands. "Look at you," she said, choosing the words she knew would hurt him. "Just look at you, in your stinking pants and your bare feet, daring to tell me what's wrong with my life. I'm sorry I let you into my car. I was sorry for you, that's all. I pitied you."

Joseph turned his shoulders away from her as if he could ward off the words. "I meant no harm," he said. "Don't be mad at old Joseph. He's just a poor old fool, a lonely old fool, doesn't know when to shut up."

Kate bent and slowly gathered up the clothes she'd dropped. Don't cry, don't cry, she stood straight again.

Joseph waited motionless, his shoulders still twisted away from her. She pushed the clothes into his hands. "Take these, please. Go in the bathroom and clean up. I can't let you go out in your wet clothes."

With his right hand he touched the inside seam of one pant leg, fumbling at the dark stain. "I meant no harm," he said again.

"Neither did I," Kate said. "I'm sorry, Joseph. I spoke without thinking. I'm sorry."

Before he could answer, she went into the kitchen and closed the door between the two of them and leaned her forehead for a moment against the satiny wood.

In the refrigerator, Kate found a package of cheddar cheese and a jar of mustard. She took two slices of bread from the freezer and dropped them into the toaster. Simple acts like these always calmed her, reassuring her with their dailiness. She could hear Joseph moving around in the living room, but she concentrated on cutting perfect identical slices from the cheese and spreading a thin glaze of mustard across the toast. She imagined Joseph going into the bathroom, washing his hands, splashing warm water against his face, admiring the way he looked in Paul's chamois shirt. She would wait, give them both a little time to rebuild their defenses.

But when she went into the pantry for a plate, she saw a dark form—it could only be Joseph, who else could it be—walking down her driveway, moving steadily away beneath the white, arched branches of the trees. He walked slowly, head tilted stiffly downward to the left, out-turned feet pushing through the snow like wooden blades.

In the living room, Kate found Paul's clothes draped neatly across the ottoman. She refolded them and put them away in their bottom drawer. Then she ate the sandwich she'd made for Joseph and listened to the tap-tap of an icy branch against the kitchen window and the slow tick of the grandfather clock. She needed suddenly to be outside, to let the snow melt against her face.

She found her warm boots and a heavy coat of Paul's and walked out to the road.

Joseph's footprints along the driveway were already faint, filling quickly with blown snow. Kate reached the paved road and then the place where Joseph had lain. Among the bushes and briers, she found her red parka buried in the snow. The coat was stiff and frosted with ice, all the warmth gone out of it, but she reclaimed it from the woods and carried it home.

Gladly, Silently, Never

I AM A TALL MAN, thinning brown hair allowed to grow shaggy around my ears, brown eyes—sad eyes, people tell me—and shoulders that curve slightly forward as if protecting something within my chest. Tonight, I wear my usual gray suit and over it a trench coat, tan in color, spotted lightly with rain. I am in a restaurant—opened just last week, best martini in San Francisco—and I stand at the bar with two young women. They are my grad students, old enough to have a drink, certainly, but too young for martinis with a middle-aged professor poet. Little I care; simply being here distracts me from the insistent loneliness that I have brought upon myself by attending more to words than people.

I raise my drink to my lips, watching the olives sway across the bottom of the glass and anticipating the first mouth-puckering taste of gin. Before I drink, someone touches my arm. I turn to see a man, so familiar I almost know him, but no, not quite. He says my name, Alan, and then his own, Daniel. His hand still on my arm, he points back across the crowded room to a table where three people sit, watching our encounter. Two of them I have never seen before. The other, his sister, I recognize only after Daniel says, "You remember Solange," and leads me to the table.

The beautiful proportion of her eyes and nose is there, but contracted somehow, so that I seem to be looking through the wrong end of a telescope. Solange rises, takes my hand, leans toward my cheek. An air kiss, no touch of lips to skin. I see that her eyes are still the color of the ocean. She is slim, taller than I remember, a graying, graceful woman dressed in something dark and plain. Her hair, cut shorter than mine, makes a smooth and shining cap around her face. She wears earrings, small, a diamond in each ear, no other jewelry.

I remember when she pierced her ears. She did it on a dare one Sunday afternoon, following directions sent by a friend. "You will need a cork, a needle, alcohol, plain earrings to wear until the holes have healed." Four or five of us were there, her roommate and two friends of mine, all seniors, fighting off mid-winter blues. Solange handed me the cork and showed me how to hold it firm against the back of her earlobe. The needle would penetrate her flesh and then the cork, making a clean hole. She sat in a chair and leaned back against me and pressed the needle through. I had expected blood, but there was none.

Thirty years.

She cannot know the many places my mind has carried her, my unseen companion, absent other. I have been married, divorced, hired, fired, published, rejected, tenured, and anthologized, most of it without her knowledge. I have devoted myself to poetry, letting wife and daughter and friends drift from me. I live alone. I drink too much. I write and, to support my writing, teach. I have created at last a restless, solitary peace. And, yet, here is Solange. I feel as if everything has shifted. Time seems infinitely past, infinitely rearrangeable.

Tonight, because the restaurant is very full, I sit at her feet on a small step that leads from one level of the room to the next. My position seems oddly familiar. I remember a spring evening— more likely it is many spring evenings folded into one. The late night air was soft, low lights hovered along campus paths, the stone steps of the library were dark and private. Sitting one step

Gladly, Silently, Never

beneath her, I courted her with poetry. The poem—it was my own, written just that afternoon—was filled with incantation, breath-pent pauses, echoes of Eliot and Joyce. Solange listened gravely, watching my face. Even then I sensed the impossibility of love.

Now, in the din of the restaurant, she leans close to me. "I'm writing a lot," she says. "Stories mostly."

How strange, I think, for her to start writing so late when words have been everything to me. "What do you write about?" I ask.

She hesitates, then, "Me. Don't you write about you?" She knows I do. Years ago, I sent her all my poems, most of them celebrations of moments, places, people we both knew.

Although so many years have passed, I still know the parameters of her life. Orphaned through twin tragedies of divorce and death, she lived with her grandmother in an ample house near a harbor full of yachts. The wind blew through the house warm and salty all day, stirring the pale curtains in the guest room where I slept alone that summer, the summer we graduated from college, the summer I followed her home.

One windy day, she took me sailing far out from the land in a little boat with two white sails. I imagined my drowned and bloated body spiraling down through dark water. Solange was showing off, telling me with her skill that she was beyond my reach, but at the same time wanting me to admire her, holding out to me the unattainable prize: herself.

"I should marry you," I said, pretending I didn't mean it and knowing my words would please her.

Inevitably, she married someone else, a teacher, a man who lived comfortably in what Solange must have seen as the real world: influential people, golf, frivolous conversation. Her husband is dead now, three years ago, a sudden aneurysm. Solange tells me this as I sit by her feet in the crowded restaurant. There are times, she says, when she is lonely, but her life is very full. Friends, two grown children, a garden—and of course her writing. She lives alone near Palo Alto. I must visit. She finds a matchbook on the table and prints her phone number inside the cover. "Call me," she says. I remember how she has always needed to be loved, hungry and elusive as a feral kitten.

When her brother and his friends stand up, she and I stand too. She kisses me this time, lips quick and moist against my cheek. "Please call," she says and goes with her brother into the rain. I watch, but she never pauses, does not look back at me. I return to my young students at the bar. I will not follow Solange, will not call or visit; I am done with loving fiercely.

"Someone from your past?" one of them asks. She has ordered second drinks for all three of us. I put down money for the bill.

After our meeting in the restaurant, Solange and I write to each other, not often, perhaps two or three letters every year. I do not phone or visit because I do not trust myself, but I send her the best of my new poems. She sends photographs of her children. I look at her daughter, searching for Solange's face, but never finding it although her daughter is not much older than we were when we met.

Solange. I might have missed her entirely if we had not shared a senior poetry seminar. The class was small, just ten students and the professor. We gathered twice a week around a rectangular table in an overheated basement classroom. The radiators on the tea-colored wall hissed steam and the fluorescent lights wavered. We were encouraged to speak up, to challenge each other on questions of poetry and scholarship. Our discussions were heated and arcane. When Solange had something to say, she raised her hand tentatively and made carefully thought out points. Her voice was steady, but I saw how, as she spoke, a deep blush flared across her cheeks and down her neck.

I began to watch her closely and came to believe that she,

like me, must hear the music of a higher sphere. I decided then to love her. It did not matter if she loved me back; I was a poet, unreciprocated love my personal muse. I followed Solange.

And she? She let me shadow her, soaking up my attention, thirsty for my adoration, gently making me know there was no hope, yet willing to go for long walks and picnic lunches, sometimes to a movie or a concert. And when I followed her home that summer after graduation, she seemed glad for the company and let me stay although, to her, we were never more than friends.

After the summer, we both went to Harvard, and so the strange symbiosis of our lives continued. Solange went to the Ed school; I was a graduate student in English literature, my course already set toward poet, professor, intellectual. I wrote my poems and read them sometimes to Solange. Solange did her practice teaching and told me how the students, seventh and eighth graders, frightened her. When we both had too much work to do—for me, a thesis, and for her, compositions to grade and student comments to write—we met in Harvard Square and studied together at a little table in the Hayes & Bickford. One late night, Solange reached across the table toward me, and I saw tears in her eyes. "I spent my entire childhood trying not to attract attention," she said, "and now every day I stand up in front of forty teenagers and try to get them to care about adverb clauses and the pluperfect."

At her invitation, I went once to watch her teach. A class on grammar and the parts of speech. If she was afraid, her students could not have known. She stood tall and composed in front of the blackboard, calling on her students confidently, commanding their attention. She had written the eight parts of speech on the blackboard in careful blue chalk.

"Look," she said, drawing a chalky circle around noun and verb. "These are the ones you want to pay attention to. The noun is the thing, the person, the physical object, the idea. The verb is everything that happens.

"All the rest," she said, drawing an X through pronoun, "are just helpers. He, she, his, yours, mine...they're nothing but understudies for the nouns. They fill in when the nouns are busy somewhere else. And these others," she Xed them out, "they're nothing without nouns and verbs." She looked expectantly at her class. From my seat in the back of the room, I saw her as a doe, ready to run, perfectly balanced between fear and grace.

Last December, I mailed Solange a Christmas card. I send one every year, the message meaningless and much the same. "Hope all is well. Give me a call sometime."

In February, Solange's brother phoned. He thanked me for the card, said he was calling for his sister. "How is she?" I asked, wondering why Daniel had called, not she. A few health issues, he told me, but she is doing well. A little lonely. I must visit soon. He gave me her address though I knew it already.

Finally, Daniel said what he had called to tell me: Solange has had a little stroke. A visit from me will cheer her up. She is eager to see me, he is certain.

I go, of course. I am needed, have been summoned. On a sunny afternoon, I drive past Palo Alto to Los Altos Hills and find her house, a dark bungalow on a quiet street. A woman in a nurse's uniform lets me in and leads me to a shaded porch that overlooks a long valley filled with fruit trees. Solange is seated in a teak armchair. When she turns toward me, I see that she is translucently thin, but there are bright pillows at her back, and on the table beside her a pitcher of lemonade, two glasses, a plate of cookies, a book of poems—my poems. She gives me her hand. It is cool and veined in blue, time ticking visibly through it. She smiles, her same smile but in a sunken face.

"She has some problems with speech," the nurse says. "Aphasia, but we think it will pass. And," the woman adds, "she understands everything we say to her. Right, honey?"

"Certainly," Solange replies. Her voice is clear and strong.

I remember her grandmother and the sound of small waves in summer.

"I'll leave you two to talk," the nurse says. I have the feeling she is escaping something troublesome, but I pull another chair close to Solange's.

"Soon," Solange says, gesturing toward the lemonade, so I pour two glasses and hand one to her. "Sweetly," she says.

"I see you have my book." I touch its cover. "I would have sent you a copy, but I've been so busy with my teaching."

"Nevertheless…" She shakes her head. I feel reproached.

"Well, of course, I should have sent it. I think you'll find bits of yourself in a few of the poems."

"Sometimes."

"Yes, well." I pause. "You know how I felt about you. It's no surprise you still creep into my poems. Especially now, now that I am looking back and almost never forward."

"Sadly. Inevitably."

Her silence makes me talkative. "I found myself flooded with memories as I drove over here, as if suddenly I was in contact again with long-buried parts of myself." Solange watches me with care. "Do you remember," I ask, "how you took me sailing once? You were so calm, and there I was, scared to death, thinking the boat would tip at any moment and I would surely drown."

She reaches for a cookie and bites precisely into it. I wait while she chews and swallows. She still wears diamonds in her ears, and even on this warm day her dress is dark and wraps around her. I expect her to say something, about sailing perhaps, or about how foolish I had been to be frightened. When she says nothing, only looks at me, I talk on.

The nurse reappears. "Everything okay out here?".

"Always," Solange tells her with a dismissive wave of one hand. "Assuredly."

"Adverbs," the nurse says perplexingly and leaves us.

When the nurse has gone, I touch Solange's hand. "I always

wished that you and I had run away," I say. "I wished we had escaped to a place where we could sit in the shade and read poetry and drink from tall glasses of rum and fruit juice."

She smiles and bends slightly toward me. Her eyes are still the same sea green.

My words slip out before my mind can stifle them. "I asked you once to marry me, do you remember?" I watch her. She is waiting. "If I asked again, what would you say?"

Now I am waiting.

"If only," she says, and covers my hand with hers. "Gladly," she says.

Her skin is very soft, and I would like to kiss her hand just there, where the narrow bones fan from wrist to fingers. Silently, we look out across the valley and the trees. I understand that we have wasted all our nouns and verbs; that we can never bring them back.

Reply in Blue

WHEN BEING UP SO HIGH, up under the highest eaves, got too much for her, Helen stopped painting. She lay the brush across the open paint can, leaned her head against the ladder and held on with both hands until she could breathe normally again. This time she froze there so long that one-eyed Merle came over from the store and scared her half to death by speaking from the foot of the ladder. "Missus," he asked, "you okay?" She nodded, though she knew he couldn't see her head. "You're standin' there so long, I thought maybe you was sick."

Helen kept her eyes shut. It was important not to look down. "I'm okay, Merle, thanks. Just taking a break."

"Queerest way to paint a house I ever seen," he offered. Then he shuffled back to his chair in front of the store. She could hear his feet on the gravel.

When he was gone, she opened her eyes and began again. For about the hundredth time that summer, Helen told herself the story of the fishermen of Burano, Italy, and how each of them paints his house a different color so he can recognize it from far out at sea. It distracted her from her fear of heights and reminded her that she was doing this for Tom.

Helen liked Tom as soon as she danced with him at the Tri-County Educators' Holiday Event. She liked his broad, sure hands and the careful way he looked at her when she spoke.

She liked his lean body and how he insisted that woodworking and poetry were the same.

Tom was nearly thirty, full of energy and optimism. Helen was twenty-five, recovering from the precipitous end of a romance, and wondering where life would carry her next. For now, she could drift along in Tom's gentle slipstream.

"Opposites attract," their friends said. Or, "You look so good together." Tom, smiling, would reach for Helen's hand. Helen, however, was awash with conflicting perceptions. "Don't push me," she wanted to say. "You don't know anything about it."

Even after Helen moved her clothes and her two cats to Tom's place (away from the road, safer for the cats), she kept her apartment and stopped there every few days to check for mail or messages. "That's so silly," Tom said. "Why pay double rent?"

"I like to be my own person," Helen countered. "And what if you get tired of me? Or discover you're allergic to cats?"

"Think about it," he said. "If we put our salaries together, we could buy a house. It's short-sighted not to own real estate, not to build up equity."

"The cats are all the equity I can handle right now."

The place in South Dennis was one of those tall, skinny New Jersey houses that looked as if someone set it down temporarily on cinder blocks and then forgot about it. Years ago the house had been white. Now it was streaked with rusty brown, the color of standing water in the cedar swamps. The house looked sad, worn down-and-out by all the lives that had passed through it.

As soon as they pulled onto the ragged lawn, Tom jumped out of the car leaving the engine running and the driver's door open. He peered into the house. Helen slid across the seat, turned off the engine, and got out of the car. Tom turned to her eagerly, "I guess this is what they mean by fixer-upper."

"Pretty grim."

"You think so? I like the trees—they're black walnuts."

"They're okay."

"Price is right."

Helen watched him prowl around the house. He was like a little kid sometimes—worse than her second graders.

"I bet the roof leaks," she said.

"Come 'round back so we can see the kitchen."

They found a window half covered with a torn paper shade. Through it they saw an old refrigerator with the door propped open and on the floor a lot of dark linoleum.

There were two other rooms downstairs, one on each end of the house with a narrow staircase running up between them. The front door opened to a screened porch where two Adirondack chairs faced the yard. Beyond the walnut trees, a shabby brown building with gas pumps in front proclaimed MERLE'S MARKET above its door. A quiet country road divided the house from the store, but even this early in the season Helen could hear the hum of Sunday afternoon beach traffic over on Route 9.

"Great porch," Tom said. "We'd sit out there all the time in summer."

"Make sense, Tom. It's a wreck."

Instead of answering, Tom went to the car and backed it close to the porch. He climbed onto the car roof and from there to the roof of the porch. He tried a window, straining to lift it until it yielded with protesting squeaks. "Come on," he called down.

"No way. I'm not climbing on that roof."

Just thinking about going up there made her breathless. Ridiculous to imagine she, of all people, would climb onto a steep roof slippery with leaves and old moss. "I'll look at the store," she told him.

Merle's Market was dimly lit and smelled of kerosene and burlap. An old man with only one eye sat behind the counter. He watched Helen but said nothing until she carried two Cokes and a bag of chips to the register.

"Lookin' at the old Foster place, eh?"

"We saw the ad in the paper, but the real estate lady didn't have time to show it today."

"I s'pect she's got bigger fish to fry."

Helen paid for sodas and chips and carried them to the house. Tom was standing in the open back door. "Come on, it's neat." She handed him his Coke and glanced around the kitchen: the refrigerator, a sink, two stoves—one a small gas stove, the other an ancient wood stove with chrome trim on the oven door and a warming shelf above the burners. Tom opened the firebox and poked at the ancient ashes. "I think it still works," he said. "We can cook dinner and stay warm at the same time."

"Regular pioneers, huh?"

"Oh come on, Helen. A little paint, a little wallpaper..." He took her hand and led her into the next room. "Here's the dining room. They left us the table."

"But no chairs. Maybe they burned them in the stove last winter."

He ignored her crankiness, urging her on to the living room. "This room will be sunny all morning. You could keep your plants in that window."

"No bathroom?"

"Upstairs. Two rooms and a bathroom with a big old tub." He bounded two-at-a-time up the stairs. Helen followed slowly. On either side of the narrow landing there was a small, dark bedroom with sloped ceilings and one window high in the wall.

"I could put skylights in. They'll be good for air circulation, and we can watch the stars from bed."

"You mean this, don't you?"

"We'll have the whole summer to work on it." He put his hands on her shoulders and looked extra serious. "Come on, Helen, say you'll help, say you'll live here with me."

"It seems like so much to bite off."

"Helen. I'm not trying to push you into anything. I'm just asking you to try it, okay?"

The closing was at the end of May. Tom and Helen moved in as soon as their schools were out for the summer, and they spent the next two months working on the house. The old man with one eye set a chair out in front of the store so he could watch. Helen talked to him sometimes while Tom worked. He had known the Fosters when they lived there. "Good people," Merle liked to say. "You and the mistah, you're good people too."

Tom bought an extension ladder and spent most of his time on the roof. He pulled off old shingles, cut holes for skylights, replaced flashing and gutters, and put on new dark gray shingles. "Come up and help," he said to Helen. "It will go much faster with two of us."

"We have all summer," she reminded him. "And you know I hate ladders." She didn't even like watching Tom up there, though she didn't tell him that. Finally he went out to Sears and bought an aluminum safety bar to make the ladder more stable.

"No," Helen said. "I'm afraid."

While Tom thumped around and sang to himself on the roof, Helen scraped and painted the interior window and door frames. She pulled up the sticky linoleum in the kitchen and flung it into the trunks of their cars. She and Tom each made daily trips to the town dump. In the evening they sat on the porch with the cats and listened to the cars on Route 9. At night they watched the stars from bed. Helen had to admit that she felt identifiably happy.

As the days got shorter and colder, their routine changed. The dining room table became the place where they corrected papers and planned lessons.

Sometimes they read aloud to each other, favorite stories or poems, or Tom told again about the fishermen of Burano. Sometimes Tom looked at Helen while they were working or reading. "I feel married to you," he said. "I love being here with you."

"Me too," she answered.

By the end of November, they had painted the front rooms white and the kitchen a pale yellow and put down a new floor of linoleum tiles. Helen was finishing the trim in the bedrooms. She'd already ordered the paper, tiny blue roses for their room and—Tom's suggestion—tiny yellow ones (gender-free, he said) for the other room.

Helen began to worry about Christmas. What could she give Tom that would measure up to the things he gave her? He liked to surprise her with gifts at odd times for no occasion at all, and he always presented them with great ceremony. She would open up a carefully wrapped box and find inside it one perfect seashell, or a poem, or a packet of catnip seeds, and once a dozen eggs from the organic farm down Route 9. Faced with so many acts of love and imagination, Helen felt helpless. A pair of socks, a shiny new hammer, a plate of homemade cookies would be inadequate as gifts for Tom.

Then in the first week of December, Tom's mother mailed them a box of family pictures, and Helen knew what to do about a present. On Christmas morning, she gave Tom a framed black-and-white, eight-by-ten photograph. Tom, age seven, grinned out at the world, knees dirty, one shoe untied, two front teeth missing. A five-year-old Helen stood beside him in a white sundress, white shoes and lacy socks. She squinted into the sun, and her cowlick stood up like a question mark.

"Where on earth?"

"The computer lab at school. Remember the pictures your mother sent? Scanned me into your picture."

"It's perfect."

"And we're exactly in character, aren't we?"

"That's the best part." Tom carried the picture over to the table by the window. He stood back and admired it. "What a hoot," he said. "Our kids are going to love that one."

Helen didn't know what to say. If it hadn't been Christmas morning, she might have told him that she was too selfish to be a mother, that it didn't matter what color wallpaper they used in the second bedroom. But it would be silly to start on that when they were supposed to be celebrating.

Tom handed her a flat, rectangular package. It weighed almost nothing. "Not your real present," Tom said, "more just an idea."

Inside Helen found five color charts for exterior house paint. Tom had put neat check marks beside the colors he liked. "We need to think about colors. It'll be warm soon, and we can work outside again. Do you like them? I've always wanted a blue house." He took the cards from her hands and began pointing at the little squares of color. "I was thinking sort of a quiet blue like that one, Summer Blue, or maybe that's too bright. Maybe this one, Dove Blue."

"I hadn't really thought," Helen said. "I promise I will."

Tom asked in January if she would marry him. He asked again in March and in April. In May, he brought home a puppy, a fuzzy mutt from the Rescue League. The puppy tried to play with the cats until they fluffed up and hissed at him. Then he chewed the leg off one of the new dining room chairs. "If this is supposed to make me want kids," Helen told Tom, "it's not working."

In June, during dinner, Tom asked again, and when Helen said her usual piece about not being ready, he pushed his chair away from the table and let it fall backwards onto the floor. The cats fled from the room. Helen sat frozen at the table. "Damn you, Helen," Tom said and went out to his car and drove away. He didn't come home that night, but the next day when Helen got back from cleaning out her classroom for the summer, the puppy was gone and a letter was propped between the salt shaker and the dictionary.

Helen—

I'm sorry. I want to share my life with you, but you don't want that. Or if you do want it, you don't want it yet. I need to think. Which will be easier if I am not with you. I will probably drive back to Boulder and see some mountains and some friends.

I love you.
Tom
(The pup's with me.)

Helen went upstairs and looked in the closet. Tom's school clothes were there, but no jeans, no work shirts, no sneakers. She looked in the bathroom. No toothbrush, no shaving cream. She went into their room and lay on the bed and looked up through the skylight. The cats came and curled against her legs, and after a while she closed her eyes and tried not to think.

The next morning, Helen began cleaning. She took everything out of the cupboards in the kitchen and washed shelves, plates, spice bottles, glasses, measuring spoons. She worked as if she could erase her failure, somehow make things right again. When the floor and counters were shining, she washed the first-floor windows inside and out. Then she went into the rest of the house. In the dining room, she took all the books off the table, off the extra chair with the chewed leg, and off the floor. She put them neatly, alphabetized by author, into the shelves that Tom had built between the front windows.

The picture of the grinning boy and the scowling girl in white mocked her. She should have known Tom couldn't be her salvation forever, that sometime he had to wear down, get tired of dragging her and all her doubts around with him.

When she had cleaned every room, she got out the paint cards with Tom's neat check marks on them. Dove Blue, she decided and drove to the hardware store before she had time to change her mind.

Reply in Blue

She started painting at ground level, beside the kitchen door, and moved counterclockwise around the house, reaching as high as she could without leaving the ground.

For the next level, the kitchen stepladder was tall enough. After that, she needed Tom's big ladder.

Once she started to paint the upper parts of the house, Helen found that moving the ladder was almost as difficult as climbing it. Helen was small, the ladder big, and its feet caught in the grass and gouged up hunks of dirt as she dragged it along another few feet. She had already been twice around the house and was finishing the highest peaks above the bedroom windows. As she climbed up and down the ladder, she inspected her work. Close up, there were places where a second coat would help. But once she was safe on the ground and could back off a little, the house was wrapped flawlessly in blue.

By afternoon, there was only one half of one triangle of white left to paint. Helen climbed down and lowered the ladder, then dragged it over to the final section and hauled the extension up again. She was getting good at going up and down, at hanging her paint can from the special loop that fit over the rung. She carried her scraper and her caulking gun in the pockets of her carpenter pants. Her back and arms were very tan, her fingernails caked with blue. She had blue freckles across her cheeks. Today a slash of blue ran from chin to ear and into her hair.

For the last time, she came down the ladder. She hammered shut the paint can, cleaned the brushes, and put everything into the shed. She leaned the ladder on its side against the back of the house. The sun was setting and the bugs were coming out, but Helen walked into the front yard and lay down between the two black walnut trees. Her arms and legs ached and her neck was stiff. She felt strong and peaceful.

There was nothing left except to wait. Sooner or later, Tom would come back, maybe tonight, maybe next month. When he did, he would see their blue house and understand that she was ready now.

Helen started to count the stars as they came out. Over on Route 9 she could hear the beach traffic heading home. She listened as the earth spun her and Tom and one-eyed Merle and all the fishermen of Burano through the heavens.

Comfort Me with Lies

"COME ON, HECTOR," I said, "We're going out." He gave me a funny look, cocking his head to one side as if he wanted to ask a question. I slipped the feather-tether harness and leash on him so he couldn't fly off my shoulder, and was already outside locking the front door when the phone started. I knew it was Lauren, but I went down the steps and along the sidewalk. I am a perfectly intelligent, grown woman, and I refuse to be treated like a baby, not even by my own sister. That's what I'll tell her next time.

It's not as if her phone call forced me from the house; I was planning to go out anyway, Hector and me. We have a favorite restaurant—Alessandro's—just a few blocks away. In winter it's a smoky little place. I don't like it and would never expose Hector to secondhand smoke, but in summer Alessandro expands his business to an outside courtyard with round tables and bright yellow umbrellas. Hector and I go there two or three times a week. The cooks and the waiters know us and come outside when they have time for a little conversation, maybe bring a special treat for Hector. These people are our friends, even though, if you asked my sister, she'd say I don't have any friends. Alessandro is our friend too. If the restaurant is not busy, he often sits with us and has a beer. Alessandro tells me about his childhood in beautiful Brazil—or did he maybe say Peru? Anyway, I ask him about Machu Picchu and the rain forest, and I tell him how I've fixed up my house for Hector and how Lauren thinks I am losing my mind.

Tonight, Hector and I are the first customers. I scrunch in

my open-toe sandals across the fine gravel of the courtyard and take the usual table. By the time other people arrive, we are seated inconspicuously in the corner near the kitchen, which is good because it keeps Hector from commenting too loudly about the other diners. Last week there was a fat woman eating ice cream. When Hector saw her, he said, "Piggy piggy oink oink." I apologized, and the woman claimed not to have understood a word Hector said. Later, I also apologized to Alessandro, who said not to worry, have another wine, but he hoped I would try not to drive his customers away.

Sometimes when Alessandro joins us, Hector and I stay until the restaurant closes for the evening. Usually, though, I leave before then because of the mosquitoes. The mosquitoes come out just around dusk, in spite of the little smudge pots Alessandro sets between the tables. Last week a waitress tripped over one of the smudge pots and fell. Sparks went up in the air and showered down on top of her. Those nylon uniforms burn like crazy, so I grabbed my water glass and emptied it onto the fallen waitress. I don't know if that's what saved her, but she laughed and thanked me and said how quick-witted I was. Later that evening, Alessandro came outside and admitted I was right about the smudge pots being dangerous.

I order a nice white wine and a cheeseburger and a plate of fruit and crackers. The wine and the cheeseburger are for me—I like the burger medium rare with fried onions and a little lettuce and a slice of tomato on top. The fruit and crackers are for Hector. Tonight, he is very interested in my potato chips. He stands on the table and picks one chip off my plate. I let him eat it even though too much salty food is bad for him.

Some nights Hector gobbles every bit on his plate, other times he just turns up his nose and looks off into the rose bushes where the feral cats live and he won't take even a single grape when I offer it to him.

Comfort Me with Lies

Alessandro encourages the cats. He puts food out for them every night, and he's bought three of those plastic igloo doghouses to shelter them from bad weather. Now and then, I try to lure the cats over to our table with little scraps of cheeseburger. I know Alessandro cares about the cats, and I want to show him I appreciate his generous and affectionate nature. I also know that Hector mistrusts the cats. "Don't be afraid, Baby," I tell him. "I'll keep you safe."

I've known Hector a long time. He lived with my Dad for years and years and had complete run of the house, so he's very set in his ways. I think Hector was part of the reason that Dad never found another wife after Mom moved out and took Lauren and me with her. That November when Dad died, it seemed only natural for Hector to move in with me. Hector speaks with Daddy's voice and sounds exactly like him. I love it, but sometimes I admit it's a little eerie to hear my father's voice when he's been dead three years. Lauren said adopting Hector was a dumb idea and I should find a more appropriate home for him, but I paid no attention. My house is plenty big enough, especially now that my husband Charleton has moved out, which is another thing that Lauren doesn't like—she can't imagine a woman being happy without a man in her life. "It's just not natural," she tells me, but I don't care what she thinks, it's my life, not hers. After Charleton left, I sold the antique bamboo furniture from the sun room and replaced it with big ficus trees and potted rhododendrons. Hector loves that room. In the summer I put the screens in so that he can whistle and call to everyone passing along the street. His whistling is a little obnoxious, I admit, but most of my neighbors know it's just Hector. Some of them whistle back. Yesterday Hector and Mr. Pacheco had a long conversation, all whistles, not a single word. I was in the kitchen putting up the clean curtains, and I couldn't believe my ears. Mr. Pacheco, the neighborhood grouch, acting so playful!

I like to keep the house clean. You wouldn't expect it to get that dirty, just me and Hector there, but you'd be amazed at how much work it is to live with Hector. Washing the curtains is just the tip of the iceberg. I wash the curtains from a different room every week, which turns out well because there are eight rooms—I complete the whole cycle in two months, then I start again. The curtains are machine washable, so the only hard part is ironing them. I turn on the TV while I iron, which Hector likes—he's always liked television, the music most of all, I think. My Dad used to watch a lot of television, and Hector sings along with the bright, chirpy tunes in the ads or before a special show.

On Monday, Wednesday, and Friday morning when I work at the Animal Hospital, I leave the TV or the radio on so Hector won't get lonely. I tell people this, and they say "how thoughtful," but I get the feeling they think I'm crazy to worry about how Hector spends his time when I'm away. But I do worry about him, and I'm always happy to get home and find him waiting. Before Hector, I had nice furniture and pretty little china figurines along the mantle and lacy shades on my lamps, but I don't mind, really I don't. Hector's company is worth more than a bunch of pretty decorations, even if they did belong to my mother's mother and I had to fight Lauren tooth and nail to get them.

The job at the Animal Hospital is dull, but I believe that working keeps me young. I answer the phones, send out bills, check the orders of supplies and medicine and pet foods when they come in. I like the people who work with me, especially Susannah, who runs the front desk. She's young, not much older than Lauren's oldest, but she's patient like a saint with all the people and their special demands. Susannah has taught me how to comfort people—tell the lie they want to hear, absolve them of all responsibility. I've seen how well it works, how thankful people are when she sets them free. "Oh, but he's had such a wonderful life," she'll say, "you're making the right decision." Or "It seems cruel, I know, but Snookie will thank you once we pull out all those bad teeth." I have also learned some First Aid, which is always good to know.

Whether you're dealing with people or animals, the basic rules seem more or less the same.

Not that I mean to say Hector is human. Obviously he's not, he's a parrot—an exceptional parrot but a parrot nonetheless. Daddy always treated him as if he were human, so I do the same thing. No one except Lauren—and Charleton, I suppose—seems to mind and nobody has ever complained at Alessandro's, though they might if we tried to go inside. In fact, there are always at least two or three people who come up and talk to us during our dinner. Some of them have really stupid questions, like "Is that a bird?" Other people are smarter. They want to know what's his favorite food, or his favorite word, or things like that. And everybody says how great he looks. That makes me feel good, because taking care of Hector is a lot of work. Between his beauty routine and mine, there's hardly a minute left in the day.

Please don't think my life centers completely on Hector. In summer, yes, Hector and I go out a lot because the weather is friendly and the days are long, but I know I need to keep up with human contacts. In winter I settle down to a real program of socialization and self-improvement. Two nights a week, I do water aerobics with a group of women whom I consider friends. I also go to a weight lifting program at the Y and a furniture repair class at the vocational school. The weight lifting—Weights for Woman—is only once a week, but it helps me stay slim and strong. The furniture class—six men, all older, and two women—meets twice a week. Our teacher, a sweet young man named Lenny, is a perfectionist and tries to make us all perfectionists, too. We scrape and sand, and then he comes around and points to the places we have missed. Then we sand again, until finally Lenny lets us do the steel wool part and begin putting on the new finish. In winter, those classes take up every weeknight, plus my three mornings at the Animal Hospital, plus shopping and cooking and cleaning the house. You can't imagine how the feathers get everywhere.

As you can see, I keep busy. I am *not* a lonely old hermit in spite of what my sister says. Lauren thinks I should move in with her and Ernest and their three kids. Lauren says she and Ernest worry about me now that I am getting older, but I am only eight years ahead of her, and most days I don't feel a bit old. Also, I think Lauren's jealous because I have Hector to remind me of our father, and she doesn't have anything. That's always been a sore point.

It's no secret I was Dad's favorite, and Lauren never forgave me. Much as she claims to care about me—"What if you fall?" she's always saying, "What if you break your hip? What if someone robs your house?" She hardly ever visits or even telephones. Now and then she has sudden inexplicable fits of trying to reshape my life, but those don't last for more than a few weeks and then she loses interest again. I don't trust her, and if you want the truth I am just as happy not to see her.

She's been on a real tear for the last couple of days because of that Sunday night when I was washing the living room ceiling. I like to scrub the ceilings at least twice a year, and I'm always careful with the stepladder, but last weekend I had a bad fall. *Wham*, right down, the ladder folds up, soapy water, scrub brush, rags, everything scattered, the ladder on top of me, the water soaking into the carpet, and Hector flying around the living room saying, "Up, UP, UP." After a couple of minutes, I did get up and reassured Hector, but I had scrapes on my legs and arms and a cut on my forehead that I couldn't get to stop bleeding no matter what I did. Against my better judgment, I called Lauren and asked for a ride to the hospital. She came instantly and stayed at the Emergency Room until the doctor had stitched up the cut, so I shouldn't complain, but since then I've had no peace.

Yesterday she was after me about getting the Community Nurse to check my stitches. I told her that was really silly with me already knowing First Aid from the Animal Hospital, and then she got snippy and tearful and said I was a human being, not an animal. "Okay, okay, okay," I said, "I give up," so the nurse came this morning and told me exactly what I knew she'd say in exactly the perky little voice they all use: "Oh, you're doing just great, Miss Wilson!"

"*Mrs.* Wilson," I snapped right back at her. It's not as if I'm an old maid. I had a pretty good marriage, and I think Charleton loves me still except he can't bear to live with Hector. He tried, I admit, but Hector never liked him. Not a surprise really, because my Dad never liked Charleton, or Ernest either, for that matter. Dad used to say they were both lazy bums, good for nothing. "Lard ass," he called them. So it was no surprise when Hector said the same thing. "Lard ass," he would shout, landing on Charleton's head and pecking at his ears. "Good for nothing," he would screech, flying with wings outspread into Charleton's face. Poor Charleton. I tried setting aside different rooms—two for Hector, the rest for Charleton. That helped, but not much. Charleton was a salesman, often worked from home by telephone, and Hector hates the phone. Any time Charleton was on the phone, Hector would whistle loudly. Even if I shut him in the sun porch, he seemed to know that Charleton was phoning, and he would scream and whistle. After a month of this, Charleton told me he couldn't work from home anymore. He had rented a little office in town, he said.

Well, that was the beginning of the end. I see it now, although at the time I thought maybe it was a good thing—make Charleton seem more professional and help him concentrate on his work, instead of being distracted by the radio or the food in the refrigerator or me. In a way I do miss him, he is a nice man, and he still sends me money every month, but I must say that the romance had gone out of our lives years before Hector came.

With Charleton out of the house, I was free to turn the entire downstairs into a jungle paradise. I read books about South America and I tried to imagine the kind of place Hector might have come from. Then I recreated it for him. I keep the heat high, and

I use spritzer bottles to keep the humidity up. I take Hector into the shower with me every morning and afterwards use the blow dryer to fluff his feathers. Some evenings I play tapes of wild jungle birds and imagine myself in a beautiful tropical forest with flowers in my hair.

When Lauren called this afternoon, she wanted me to sign up for Meals on Wheels so I wouldn't have to go to the store or worry about cooking. Lauren acts as if I am 109 instead of 68, and it really makes me angry even though I am normally an even-tempered person. And do you suppose Meals on Wheels would bring food for Hector? No, he'd have to settle for a share of mushy peas or slimy green beans or god-only-knows-what-else they put in those dinners. I much prefer dining at Alessandro's, and next time Lauren calls I will just slam the phone down. I don't need her butting into my life.

But we're at Alessandro's now, and I don't want to ruin a nice evening with thinking of Lauren. I sip a little wine and scrunch around in my chair so the umbrella shades me better. You have to be careful these days about the sun, though this late in the day maybe it doesn't matter. Except, you never know, anything can happen.

I offer Hector a bit of lettuce from my cheeseburger. "Here, Baby," I say. He takes the lettuce like I knew he would, but then he lets it drop to the ground. "Hector, what's…" I start to ask. Before I can say another word, Hector flaps onto my shoulder.

"Lard Ass," he says. "Lard Ass. Thankless Bitch." Thankless Bitch was my Dad's pet name for Lauren. He always said it with affection, but Lauren never got used to it. It's not a name I ever dare use, but I trust Hector to be giving me an accurate warning. I look around for them—Lauren and Ernest. No sign, until I glance into the restaurant. Yes, of course, they'd never think of eating outside. I see Alessandro pointing toward my table, and when Lauren turns around she sees me. It's too late to flee, so

I sit as composed as I can. Here they come. Ernie really is a lard ass.

"Lock the door! Fall to the floor! No one home. No one home." That's Hector. He starts out in a quiet tone, but within about two seconds he's yelling in Dad's creaky old voice, "Lock the door! Bar the window!" Other people in the courtyard start looking at us. "Lard Ass," Hector cries. "Thankless Bitch."

Lauren and Ernie are walking towards me, and I see Alessandro standing in the doorway watching them. He looks at me and shrugs, arms out. He knows exactly how I feel about Lauren, but what else could he have done? I don't blame him for pointing me out to her.

Lauren is at my table, looming over me. Hector balances on my shoulder, wings held angrily away from his body, feathers fluffed aggressively. In a minute he will fly at her face. "Easy, Hector," I say. I smooth his feathers, scratch the back of his head.

"Gretchen," says Lauren, "we were so worried. I called back, and you didn't answer. We went to your house, let ourselves in with your secret key. I was sure I'd find you fallen again, helpless on the floor." It was that word—helpless—that cleared my head and determined my next words.

"Lauren," I said, "Ernest, I have something to tell you, something wonderful." I pause. They are listening. "I was going to wait, but you deserve to know, to be the first of all my friends to hear the happy news." Lauren stepped back from the table. She reached for Ernest's arm. Maybe I had gone too far with happy news. People at the other tables were watching our little drama. This would probably be the last night Hector and I would be welcome at Alessandro's. Alessandro himself had come up close behind Ernest and Lauren. He looked at me with a question on his face. "What can I do?"

I smiled at him and held out my hand. "Alessandro," I said, beckoning him closer. He stood beside me, and I rose and linked my arm in his.

"Lauren, Ernest, I want you to meet Alessandro. Alessandro, this is my sister, Lauren, and Ernest." Alessandro bowed to them and did not pull away from me. I didn't know if I could trust him, but I had gone too far to retreat.

"Alessandro," said Hector, "Mi querido Alessandro." At least Hector understood. "Alessandro and I are engaged," I said.

Up to this point, Lauren had not bothered to look at Alessandro. Now she did. A short, dark, middle-aged Hispanic man wearing a white apron with smears of brown grease across the front, straight dark hair, beautiful eyes. "We are in love," I said. "We will marry."

Alessandro watched me with considered interest. "Alessandro, Hector and I—in a year or two, we will move away from here. We will return to the jungle, to South America, Hector's homeland and Alessandro's."

Lauren was speechless, looking from me to Alessandro to Hector. Hector began to sing. "It's Amore," a song Daddy had taught him years ago. "Amore, amore, it's amore."

Alessandro laughed with apparent delight. I dared to kiss his cheek. What a lovely man. I imagined a hut, bamboo walls, roof of grass, Hector and his relatives gathered in low, moist trees while Alessandro and I played cards and drank nectar from tiny golden cups crafted, I was certain, by the Incas themselves.

Green

ALL THAT SHE PLANTED is growing and green, entwining the house in vines full of birds building nests. Patricia had created this mesh of green. "How lovely to have a trellis here, all along this porch," she'd told Jeffrey. "Think of summer evenings and the smell of flowers," she'd whispered to their little daughters. Although she had wanted this, she could not now remember what she'd pictured. But not this, not this web, this maze of green.

Patricia is outside, but hears her daughter in the kitchen. The Champion Grinder whirrs, the lid of the trash can opens, clangs shut. Plates clash together in the sink. In the grinder, carrots make a different sound from cucumbers—sharper, more like teeth. Sarah has come up from Brooklyn to help. She eats only raw food. Nothing killed, nothing cooked. Just chop, macerate, grind, mix. Sarah is thirty now, old enough surely to determine her own diet, but to Patricia her every food-related act seems abrupt, noisy, full of reproach. Yesterday, when Sarah arrived, she brought Patricia a raw foods cookbook. "For you, Mom," she said, holding it out with pride.

"*RAW: The UNcook Book*," Patricia read. "How interesting, Sarah. Thank you."

Sarah reclaimed the book and flipped through its pages. "They're great recipes, and easy, and maybe you'll see why I'm the way

I am." She hurried on, allowing Patricia no time to reply. "I'm giving one to Laura and David too, plus the best food mill ever. Don't you think that's a good wedding present?"

"Certainly an unusual one. And good, I guess, if you think they'll use it. "

"Laura's already half there. She won't touch red meat."

The old wooden ladder lies beside her in the grass. The secateurs—what a lovely word for a pair of shears—are in her hand. Except for the clatter of Sarah in the kitchen, Patricia is alone. They will arrive soon, wanting, asking, needing; she must not delay. Raise the ladder, almost too heavy, its long weight twisting against her strength. Lean it into the green, the leaves smothering it. The vines clasp the top rungs as if to draw the ladder into their web.

Patricia had welcomed those little shoots emerging curled like ferns in early spring, the long ago innocence of her daughters as they helped her plant and pat down the earth and water and weed. "Grow," she had wished, "thrive." How wonderful to be a family, the four of them, to have this grand old summerhouse, this lovely life. "We are so fortunate," Patricia told her husband. "Believe in goodness," she whispered to her daughters as she planted wisteria, honeysuckle, and clematis and trained the tendrils to climb.

And so it made sense when Laura and David announced at Christmas that they wanted to be married here, on the lawn. The last weekend of August, beneath the long arbor, facing the sea.

At first—Patricia admitted it to Jeffrey only—she had been surprised by their choice. For the past few years—six? eight?—neither Laura nor Sarah had spent more than hurried weekends at the island house. They had their friends, of course, Patricia understood, and jobs, other summer plans. As for Jeffrey, well, Jeffrey had his work, ever more demanding. All he managed was a week or two, usually in August, and for the past three years

Patricia had come alone, with his blessing, a month ahead of him. Free of all expectations, she spent her time in the hammock on the front porch, reading, and listening to the wind. She did not garden, did not weed, did not prune or plant. The house, once gleaming with family, grayed and leaned against the wind. Each year when Patricia arrived, she patrolled the damp rooms, finding and sweeping away papery husks of hornet nests and cobwebs that quivered in the sunlight.

Patricia and Jeffrey had talked about selling the house—his house, inherited from his mother. "We don't use it," Jeffrey would say. "It costs so much. The girls no longer come, not a surprise really, the island like a giant carnival, not how it used to be. All those rich people. And mopeds—populous and annoying as flies. We'd probably get a good price."

"We'd miss it so, you and I."

"But we could travel."

"I want the girls to feel a connection, how time reaches back in a place like this—their grandmother's house, their childhood summers, yours too. I'm not ready to abandon all those memories." And Jeffrey would nod, as if relieved, the inevitable postponed.

From the top of the ladder, Patricia sees how the vines intermingle, but she can't track them back to their roots. She leans, reaches, the branches brush her face. The wisteria has faded, leaving ugly brown pods. The honeysuckle twines everywhere, fading but still fragrant. And the clematis (because Patricia mistakenly bought the autumn bloomer) will not flower until September. For Laura's wedding, she wants it all neat, perfect, a sculptural frame for bride and groom. But the secateurs, despite their lovely name, are too big, hard to wield among the intricacy of branches:

She hears the crunch of gravel on the driveway and the slam of car doors. The boat has been on time, then. Better go down, say hello, and see what is needed. She loves these children, her niece and nephew, though their mother—Jeffrey's half-sister, Marigold—drives her crazy with that constant chatter. Secateurs beneath her arm, Patricia backs down to the foot of the ladder. She discovers Sarah waiting there. "Mom, what are you doing?"

"Trimming. I've let things go for much too long."

"You're cutting down the vines?" Sarah gestures toward the tangle of greenery around the ladder's feet. "Plants have as much right to be here as we do."

"Sarah, I'm sorry. I know how you feel; we've been through this before. But there's the wedding. I want things in order, cared for."

"The best care for the natural world is to just let it be."

"Oh, Sarah…" but Sarah has turned and is walking toward the driveway. Patricia follows. Marigold greets her with a squeal of pleasure. Hugs, kisses, the children standing back until Patricia turns their way. She bends to them, "Hello hello and welcome, are you hungry, thirsty?" They come to her; wrap cool arms around her neck and shoulders.

"Gammy, gammy," they chant, though she is not their grandmother, not really. "I have a camera," says Matthew. "It's real." He holds up a disposable Kodak. "Smile, Gammy." She smiles. "Got it," he says and runs toward the house.

Jeffrey—it was Jeffrey who met them at the boat—stands beside the car. He could almost be one of those long-legged wading birds, a blue heron hypnotized by the whirl of minnows around his feet. Patricia takes his arm and steers him toward the kitchen door.

Marigold follows. "It is so beautiful here," she cries. "I always forget and then poof, here it is again, like a miracle."

"A miracle indeed," says Jeffrey.

Patricia beckons everyone into the kitchen. "Here," she says, "I made fresh lemonade, and snickerdoodles."

"Oh, that's too much sugar for the children," Marigold says.

She reaches for the plate of cookies, lifts a snickerdoodle to her lips and nibbles dainty as a mouse.

"My favorite," says Matthew, taking two. Martha takes just one, shyly, and balances it on her palm. Jeffrey pulls out a chair and sits at the table. Sarah comes in from the hall. She has combed her dark hair and pulled it back into a long ponytail. Her face shines with virtue.

"No sugar for me, thanks," she waves the cookies away. "Come over here, Martha, and tell me a secret."

"I've been trimming the vines," Patricia says. "What a jungle. We'll need to make a dump trip tomorrow morning. I've already got a pile, though Sarah disapproves. She thinks I'm desecrating nature."

"Well, you are, but you planted it in the first place; it's yours to desecrate." That's Jeffrey.

Sarah leads Martha away. They are pure spirits, she and Martha. Martha is five and believes anything that Sarah tells her, and Sarah basks in her admiration.

"My best friend's cousin got married last month, right here on the island. Such a summer of weddings," Marigold takes another cookie. "She met her husband at a triathlon in Hawaii—the Iron Man, Iron Woman, something—and they wanted to get married during a triathlon because that's their happiest time. I never would have picked them for a couple. He's huge, all muscles, and she's tiny as a wren. I can't imagine "

"Marigold, do you mind sharing the front bedroom with your kids? We're a little tight for space with Laura and David's friends staying here."

"Oh no, anything is fine. You're a saint to have us. But anyway, they were in this race here on Nantucket, the bike part, 26 miles, I think, except he rode up to the top of Altar Rock and waited. He was ahead, of course, he's always ahead—and she stopped at the bottom of the hill, and her mother was there with a veil and a big fluffy skirt—all white, with Velcro closings."

"They dropped out of the race?" asked Jeffrey.

"Just long enough for her to Velcro on her veil and skirt and walk up the hill. The minister was there, he married them and they both went back into the race."

"Did she take off the skirt?"

"I don't know. I suppose she must have. Anyway, they finished the race, and all the racers celebrated with them. Isn't that wonderful?"

"It's almost as cheap as eloping," says Jeffrey. "I can only wish."

"Oh Jeffrey, you don't mean that." Marigold ruffles his hair. "Wow, you're losing it aren't you! My own brother, bald!"

The leaves of the vines are still wet from the morning fog that wraps the island. Patricia has found her smaller clippers in a kitchen drawer, and she begins snipping carefully, leaning back to evaluate her work. When she is done, this will be a canopy of honeysuckle and pale budding clematis. The old porch will reclaim for a few weeks its gracious past, decorous in a veil of leaves and buds. Gentle Laura will be married with beauty and tradition all around her.

I still have time, Patricia tells herself, playing out the weekend in her head. Laura and David don't come until tomorrow afternoon, Friday. The wedding is Saturday—not until 4—so she still has two full days counting Saturday. She has taken care of everything, all the planning, all the worrying. Really, there is nothing left for her to do. She and the caterer have reviewed the vegetarian options. Yesterday, with her own hands and considerable trepidation, she baked the wedding cake (carrot cake, one layer only) and assembled everything she needed for the cream cheese frosting. She hired the bartender—full bar, wine with dinner, champagne toast, and liability insurance. Jeffrey paid the band.

She has ordered the flowers—summer wildflowers, mostly weeds, black-eyed Susan and Queen Anne's lace. She has the place cards, the little gifts, the helium balloons to mark the driveway.

She wishes she had the tent, but Jeffrey has vetoed that. "Ridiculous expense. It's always sunny in August."

Matthew and Martha are in the kitchen, Sarah with them offering blueberries and homemade granola. Sarah comes to the window. "I'll entertain them, Mom, while you defy the natural world." A year ago, Patricia and Sarah would have argued over this, over the weird foods and Sarah's stringent requirements for living lightly on the earth. But lately they seemed to have reached a plateau, mutual disapproval set aside out of affection.

"Yes, please," Patricia says, "if you could just...for the morning. Take them to the windmill...Jetty Beach...ice cream on Steamship Wharf."

"I know where to go, Mom. Trust me."

Last night after dinner, they had relaxed with drinks on the long porch. The night was warm, almost tropical and full of dampness. "Muggy," Jeffrey's mother would have called it. Jeffrey and Marigold reminisced. The summer teas their mother used to give, all the round tables on the porch, pastel tablecloths, monogrammed napkins, ladies in flowery dresses and big hats. "She made it look so easy," Marigold said. "But of course that's the art of entertaining, isn't it? Making it seems simple."

"Perhaps, my dear sister, you've forgotten. There were the servants. Do you suppose our mother cut the crusts off all those tiny sandwiches herself?" While Jeffrey and Marigold chattered, Sarah instructed little Martha about the miracle of seeds. "Fruits have a seed, and that gives birth to a new tree, and the tree gives us food and shelter. Everything that people need begins with the seed."

"Sarah, please, can we plant the thing from the peach? The stone?"

"Of course. We'll find a sunny place for it."

"And next summer we get peaches!"

"Well, maybe not that soon, but someday."

"Cross your heart?"

"Cross my heart."

Patricia listened. How she loved them all, and grieved for them, their innocence. Sarah's strange amalgam of ferocity and fragility. Let them be happy. Let them be safe.

Laura and David and six of their friends came on the Friday afternoon boat. The ride over had been rough, they said. For fear of being seasick, they sat outside, on the top deck where the wind was strong. No, none of them has been to the island before. It's so beautiful, the waves were so big, what a wonderful old house.

"There's a storm coming, you know," Sarah tells them.

"A storm?" Patricia is startled. "A storm?" she asks again, but no one answers. Instead, Laura reels off the names of her friends, assigns them to rooms, and tells them how to get to the beach. They open beers and lounge on the porch. Patricia knows she'll never get their names straight so she settles for her own identification system. The skinny blond, the two brothers, the beautiful one….

Laura looks so wonderful. Happy, laughing, touching David at every opportunity. Her skin is perfect, her hair waves glossy and joyous around her face. Love has remade her.

But it is Marigold who understands. "Sweetie," she says, her arm around Laura, "you look wonderful." She pulls Laura close to her, away from the others, and lowers her voice. "Do you maybe have a secret we should know? Or should your Aunt Marigold just shut up?"

"Oh, Marigold," says Laura, "you're always the observant one."

"Sweetheart! How wonderful," Marigold reaches for David, pulling him into the circle, turning to Patricia. "Did you hear? Did you know?"

No, Patricia has not heard, did not know, not at least until this moment. When she realizes where the conversation has gone, "Laura…" is all she says, but a quick, wild spike of joy rises in her.

"I'm so happy, Mommy, but we weren't going to tell anyone yet, not till after. And guess what, my dress still fits."

The rain begins just before dawn on Saturday. Patricia wakes to the sound of it against the house and hurries downstairs to close windows and carry in cushions from the porch. Back in bed she listens to the wind. Later in the morning, she stands on the porch and observes the piles of rented tables and white folding chairs, the coiled strings of lights, the barbecue grills, and the wooden dance floor already warping at its corners.

"I just heard the weather. The boats aren't running," Jeffrey announces when he comes downstairs. "I'm glad we didn't rent a tent, it would have blown away by now."

The phone rings all morning. Marigold's husband, the cousins from Detroit, the photographer. "The boat's not running," they say. "The airport is closed."

Matthew is delighted. "I have my camera," he exclaims, "I'll take all the pictures."

The caterer has taken over the kitchen. David and his brothers have set up the rented chairs and tables along the porch, as many as will fit, the rest in the dining room. Laura and her friends have spread the tablecloths and gathered stones from the garden to hold them in place. To make room for dancing, the living room furniture is pushed back, into the corners, into the hall, into Jeffrey's study; the old Oriental rug rolled up and dragged to the second floor.

The wind increases, lashes at the house, slides the white chairs across the porch. The tablecloths fly up like kites and Patricia rushes to gather them in. One table flips over, then another, and another in a noisy chain reaction. David and his brothers capture the tables, fold them flat and stack them again on the grass. People will just have to eat standing up or huddled beneath the uncertain shelter of the porch roof. Patricia goes upstairs where Laura is getting dressed.

Laura sits on the bed, tightening the thin straps of her sandals. "Mom, the rain…"

Patricia sits beside her and with her fingertips traces the shape of her daughter's cheek. "It will be fine," she promises. "It will be wonderful, it has to be."

By half past three, the house is battened down against the storm. The band has come, four young men in boots and cowboy hats. Sarah shows them where to plug in their amplifiers and brings them towels so they can wipe water off their hair, their feet, and their instrument cases. "You'll have to make do," she tells them. "It will be a little crowded."

Laura's friend, the beautiful one, collects the vases of flowers and lines them up along the stairs. The skinny one ties the balloons to the porch railing where they batter and twist and finally break free. Arriving guests run squealing from their cars, most of them barefoot and kicking through the puddles. The Justice of the Peace comes wrapped in a purple cloak and transparent rain hat, her make-up streaked, her Bible in a plastic grocery bag. Matthew takes her picture. Marigold tells another of her wedding stories, a Lithuanian wedding last year in Montreal. "The bride and groom had to circle the altar, their hands were bound together with a silken cord, their attendants followed them and held crowns above their heads. It was all in Lithuanian, so I'm not sure what anyone said, but it was a wonderful wedding."

Jeffrey signals from upstairs that they are ready, and the band plays quietly, unplugged. Everyone gathers around the stairs. Sarah comes first, holding Martha's hand as they negotiate the stairs. They wear matching dresses of green and white flowered cotton. David's brothers follow, serious, zinnias in their dark lapels, then Jeffrey, and Laura in her long white dress.

"Who gives this bride in matrimony?" asks the Justice of the Peace.

"We do," says Jeffrey. "Her mother and her sister and I." He kisses Laura and comes to stand next to Patricia. Patricia looks for David's parents. They're divorced, but for the moment they are together. Possibly they are holding hands. Do they know yet about the baby? Patricia will not be the one to tell them, let David and Laura do that.

The lights flicker but do not blink out. There are the vows, the poem, the kiss—a real kiss, so real that Matthew forgets to take a picture. Marigold dabs at her eyes with a Kleenex. The front door stands open and the rain blows in across the porch, but no one seems to notice.

Afterwards, in the kitchen, Patricia watches as Sarah sneaks a narrow line of frosting from the wedding cake and licks it from her finger. When Sarah sees her mother, she grins wickedly and takes another fingerful of frosting. "Yummy frosting, Mom."

Laura and David come into the room. Laura is laughing, her white dress swooping behind her across the damp floor. "What a wonderful wedding," she cries. The caterers applaud, and Laura curtseys to them all.

Deersie

SUNDAY MORNING. The sun's close to comin' up, and I'm drivin' my truck, not knowing where to go, just tryin' to keep my head together and wishin' myself into yesterday, wishin' it's Saturday afternoon, and me still alone in that big old field hearin' the wind in the trees and thinkin' how good it is to get away from everyone. Away from Mama, work, work, work, never sits still a minute, away from Pops snoring in his chair, drunk maybe, I dunno, don't care. Away from my yappy sisters, four of them, never shut up, yammer yammer, yap yap. I could've stayed in that field for hours, just soak up the quiet. Could've stayed for days. Should've maybe, but how was I s'posed to know?

Saturday afternoon. I got my ass on this big rock, gray granite, pretty much flat and still warm from the sun. I'm wearin' my new camo suit, put it on over by the truck before I came down the hill. It's all splashes of brown and mucky green. No way a deer's gonna see me so long's I hold quiet. All I gotta do is wait.

Got my arrows too. Homemade. I carve 'em out myself, collect the feathers all year long. This one here's got blue jay feathers. Blue jay are best, so bright I can track the arrow through the air and see the exact moment when it hits, *whap!* and sinks through the flesh. Shit, but I love this hunting.

I make my breathing slow and quiet, like I'm some stupid scarecrow, or a dead man, even, and I hear something, rustling around real cautious at the edge of the woods. It's them, but they can't hear me, can't smell me either downwind like this. Come on, you fuzzy shits. I know you're there. I got a blue jay wants to meet you. There's a doe, right where the path comes outta the trees, deciding if it's okay.

Come out, missy, a little further, get out in the open so I can see you better. Slow, slow, slow, I fit my arrow into the bow and wait. Come on, girly, let's get this show on the road. I pull back the string, so silent and careful, my arm's barely moving. One more step, little lady, and you're someone's supper. Now? But there's another, two more. The doe looks back at them, like to say "all clear" and here they come. Except they're little. The two of 'em, tiny fucking little baby fawns. I relax my arm and slowly let the bowstring go loose so the blue jay arrow hangs down, aimed at nothin' but the ground. Lucky day for you, mama doe, wicked lucky.

But fawns? They s'posed to get born in spring, right? But here they are, screwing up my day. Like Mother Nature made another of her sick mistakes. I don't twitch a muscle, just watch the three of them. The fawns are older than they looked at first. But still they're young, too young for this time of year, too young to lose their momma. I sit and puzzle on this awhile. Who knows, what the hell, but my eyes don't lie: I'm looking at a mama deer and two barely even teenagers chowing down for the night and twitching those stupid tails.

I love it when a deer runs from me. It'll flick up its tail, bright as a big white handkerchief. Like a surrender flag. "I give up. Don't, don't, don't shoot," and then *pffttt*, gone! Except you hear it crashing through the trees. Or maybe that big white tail is like a target, like the damn deer sees you, she's teasing you. "Go ahead, waste an arrow," that tail says. "Shoot me if you can," and mostly you can't because the fucking deer's so quick, plus you don't want to hit her in the ass, not that you could. And you know, I gotta admit that seeing those tails flash is almost worth missing the shot. Not the same as hitting one and watching her go down, no way near, but it sure gets my heart banging when they run like that.

I read somewhere, I think in one of those bow hunting magazines, how a deer will always run uphill if it's not wounded bad. You can learn stuff from those magazines. There's a big bookstore at the mall, got skinny aisles, high shelves, green leather chairs. I go in lots a afternoons, like it's my own personal library. I aim to read every one a those scifi books—*Green Mar*s, *Red Mars*, *Blue Mars*—guy named Robinson, writing all crazy stuff about California. Mostly I slide into one a those big chairs, read two, three chapters, put the book back on the shelf. Or days I don't have much time, I pick up a couple magazines. There's all different stuff—bow hunting, monster trucks, surfing, whatever. I sit and flip through the pages. It's kind of like hunting; stay quiet long enough, after a while they don't even see you. When the time's right, I jam the 'zine I want inside my jacket and make a show of putting the other ones back where I got them. Then I'm out of there.

Pops would kill me if he knew, but he never notices anything. Most of the time, it's like he don't even see me. He pays attention to my sisters. Talks nice to them. Brings 'em stuff, little presents, like. Takes 'em out in the car. But never me. Pisses me off sometimes, feeling like an invisible hunk of shit, but I know it's better than him being on me all the time. Even so, my sisters don't much like him, always making faces behind his back and imitating how he walks when he's wasted. Mama barely talks to him at all, like she's forgotten how to speak. Except she talks fine when he's not around.

Saturday afternoon. No hurry to go home. I'd rather be out here, sitting on a rock while the sun goes down. The deer are still nibbling at the grass, but they're sort of shifting from one foot to another and looking around, maybe getting ready to run. I start thinking how I should've brought Lily. She's never seen a real deer, not close like this, just in my magazines. Lots of times, I let her come into my room, and I pull a couple magazines from under my mattress. I tell her she can read them even though I don't think she knows how to read, she just likes the pictures.

Mama says Lily's never gonna act any older than she does now. It's weird, y'know, cause she looks like any other girl—brown wavy hair, big smile, boobs just starting to bump out—but she acts like she's five or six 'stead of—what? twelve maybe? Around twelve, cause I remember when Rosie brought her home and told me I had a new baby sister. I was a little kid then—six years old? seven?—anyway too dumb to ask why it's Rosie, barely fifteen, who's carrying my baby sister home instead of Mama. Later on, the couple times I got 'round to ask about Lily, Mama told me shut up, mind my own business. I don't ask questions anymore, except I try to be nice to Lily when I can. I don't care if Mama's her mother or if Rosie's her mother, what's the difference? I just feel sorry for her, sorry for Rosie too, I guess.

Lily can't sit quiet more than a couple minutes, but you should see when I give her the magazines. She'll look forever at the pictures, doesn't seem to notice if the animals are alive or dead, just pats them with her stubby fat hands and jabbers. It's hard to understand what she says, she smushes words together, up and down, down and up, Lily's song, I tell her. Could be she's singing to the deer. Who knows. Too bad she can't see these guys today. Definitely alive, and so close I could almost spit on them except the wind's in my face. Lily'd love it. But I don't know, could Lily sit still all this time? More likely, she'd start waving her arms around and rocking back and forth, and next thing they'd run and she'd be saying, "Bye, bye, deersies. Bye, bye, deersies," like she does when I put the magazines back under my mattress.

Anyhow, it's all of a sudden cold out here, too cold for Lily. She gets to shivering sometimes, can't stop. If I'm cold sitting here, she'd be freezing, and I'm so cold my ass is ice. I clap my hands together two times, loud. The doe and the fawns jerk up their heads, big ears flicking like crazy. That's right, ladies. It's me, public enemy number one. Shit, but look at them run, tails up, jumping over the bushes like they're flying.

Home. Sky already dark, Pops' car in the driveway, white fence 'round the yard, couple big trees in front. I stash the camo, the bow, the arrows. Everything I care 'bout I keep in the truck. Safer here under the camper cap. Nothing's safe in the house, Daisy and Violet, they poke into everything, take what they want, steal my socks, fuckin' wear my shirts to school. "Oh," they tell their friends—I've heard Daisy say these exact words—"it's my boyfriend's shirt; he *loves* for me to wear it." I lock the truck—my truck, bought it myself, worked construction last summer, nobody drives it but me. I push my hair out of my eyes. Clump the mud off my boots. Slide in the back door, stand in the little back entryway and listen to who's where, what's up.

Pops' brown Carhartt coverup that he wears to work is hanging on the coat pegs, stiff with dirt and cement dust, still shaped just like Pops is shaped, round, thick. The suit's knees and elbows are bent, almost like Pops still inside it, except I can see him in the front room, slumped in his big recliner. By tomorrow, Mama will have that coverall washed clean and ironed flat, the shape of Pops pressed right out of it, ready for another week. Pops drives one a those big cement trucks, works every weekday and every Saturday morning. Rest of the time he's in that recliner, TV muted, watchin' guys bounce a ball, hit a ball, throw a ball, fall down on a ball.

Today Pops got the TV picture goin' and them big padded earphones jammed onto his head, curly wire running across the rug from Pops to the stereo. He looks like a fighter pilot or somethin' but actually he's listening to those fat guys—the loud singers. Two or three of them Pops says he can't get enough of. Mostly he just sits and listens, except sometimes he'll all of a sudden start singing along "Nessun dorma"—all that kind of shit. Italian, I think, something like that.

I check the stove. Something cooking, big pot, heat turned low. I grab a potholder, slide the lid back a little and have a look. Soup, some damn kind of soup. Mama puts anything she finds into soup—old cabbage, chicken bones, potatoes going soft. I don't ask anymore. Better just to eat. Looks like I'm lucky though—Mama and the rest of them nowhere around, shopping, I bet, they like shopping on a Saturday. And Pops can't hear anything 'cept the fat men, so I don't have to talk to any of 'em.

Being Pops' first and only son, I get a bedroom to myself. Daisy and Violet have to share, and Lily sleeps in with Rosie, the both of 'em in Rosie's big double bed. Couple weeks ago I put a lock on my door, but Pops made me take it off. "No secrets in *my* house," he says. So now there's a round hole where the lock used to be. I got it covered over with duck tape, don't want my sisters peekin' at me.

In my room, door shut, light on, unlace my boots. Boots get hot, heavy after a while. I like to let my feet breathe. One boot off, drop it on the floor. Start on the other, but I hear something that I shouldn't hear. It's a scratching, scrabbling kind of sound and it's coming from under the bed. I say, "Lily? Hey, Lily?" and out she comes. Faded old red dress, feet bare, face dirty and streaked with tears, cobwebs and dust in her hair. She wiggles out from under the bed and crawls up beside where I'm sitting and burrows her head into my shoulder. She's almost the same size as me, but she's got herself scrunched into a little ball.

"Hey, Lily? What's up?" She don't say a word. "Lily, you okay?" Now she shakes her head, back and forth, back and forth, smearing snot and tears into my shoulder. I reach up and put my hand on her hair, hold her head still. She goes quiet, won't look at me, keeps her face against my shirt.

Okay, I can wait, I'm good at waiting, been waiting all my life. For what, who the hell knows, just waiting. Right now, I'm waiting for Lily to calm down, forget whatever's her trouble. After about five minutes she looks at me and sort of smiles, like she's figured out I'm there and she's glad to see me. "Hi, Lilio," I say real gentle. "Boy are you dirty." I touch her cheek, but she pulls away like she's a little wildcat. "You stay here, I'm getting a towel, clean you up some." I know to use warm water, no soap. One time I got soap in Lily's eyes and did she howl.

When I'm back from the bathroom, Lily's looking out the window, down at where I park the truck. No way she can see much in the dark, but maybe she's watchin' for Mama's car, wishing she'd went with them. I hand her the wet towel. She knows what I want and scrubs the towel around on her face awhile. Then I take it back, and she lets me finish the job. I tell her about the deer—the doe and the two fawns. She points at my bed, says "deersie deersie," so I pull out a couple bow hunter magazines for her. On the cover of one of them there's a picture of a fawn. I tear that page off and give it to Lily. It's an old magazine, she's seen it a hundred times, but this is the first time I ever gave her anything to keep for herself. She holds the page in both her hands and looks at it, looks at me, looks at the page, looks at me, grins like crazy and folds the page into a nice neat square that fits perfect into the pocket of her dress.

Mama and them's back. Kitchen door slams open, slams shut. Crinkle of paper bags and the heavy dull clunk of cans against the counter. Daisy and Violet come up to their room, close the door like always. Then Lily and I go to the kitchen. Rosie's still down there, sliding the cans onto the shelves, but she stops when we come in and gives Lily a hug. "Hi, Potato Cake," she says cause she knows that'll make Lily laugh.

The kitchen's the best room in the house—big and square, two windows, dark red linoleum on the floor, open shelves that Pop built along one wall for cans and boxes and two big tins for flour and sugar. Pops used to be real good at building stuff—he's who taught me to make arrows—but it's like he don't care anymore. Mama keeps the dishes on three shelves next to the sink and her pots and pans under the counter by the stove. Right now, Mama's stirring the soup. She dumps in a can of those fat red beans, and she hands me a can of corn and the can opener.

Lily watches us put the corn in with the beans and whatever else is in the pot. Smells pretty good, and Mama's looking happier than sometimes. She's combed her hair nice for the store, put on a little lipstick. I bet Mama was real pretty when she first met Pops.

Mama yells up the stairs for the girls. Then she ladles out a bowl of soup for Pops and cuts two big hunks of bread off the loaf. She puts butter on the bread and gets a spoon out of the drawer and hands everything over to Rosie. "For your father," she says. "He can eat in there." Easier that way, we don't bother him, he don't bother Mama. The other six of us sit around the kitchen table. The soup's good, doesn't even need salt, and the bread's fresh. I keep quiet and eat, but everybody else, 'cept for Lily, is talking.

How they saw that crazy old man again out in front of the store. How the prices of everything keep going up. How Rosie's going out tonight. Rosie's been going out a lot lately, four nights already this week. "Where you go to?" Violet asks.

"The movies, sometimes. Out to eat," Rosie says.

"Then what?" Violet wants to know, and Rosie won't say, and no, she says, she won't take her sisters with her, she's meeting friends.

"Who, who, who," Daisy asks. She's like a screech owl perched in the corner of Mama's kitchen. I'm glad when Rosie tells her shut up, it's none of her beeswax. Mama doesn't want a fight, so she asks me what I did today. Daisy and Violet get up to wash the dishes—that's their job, every night. They wear green plastic gloves, don't want their nails wrecked. Stupid girls look like

Martians. Rosie goes to get ready for wherever, but Lily comes and leans against me while I tell Mama about the fawns.

If I kill a deer, I don't tell Mama anything. I just dress the carcass out and give Mama the meat, and she cooks it, no complaints. What Mama likes are the stories about the deer getting away, so I tell her how the three deer came out of the woods, how close I sat to them, how they ran with their tails flashing white. By the time I finish the telling, Lily's pulling at my arm. I know she wants to look at the magazines again, so I let her lead me upstairs and back to my room.

On the way up, we meet Rosie coming down. She's got like a little overnight bag in her hand, and she stops me on the stairs and whispers, "I won't be back till tomorrow, but don't tell, okay?" I nod, yes, like Rosie's telling me a secret, except it's a secret we all know. Rosie goes quietly down the stairs, through the living room and out the front door. That way she won't have to pass by Mama in the kitchen.

Lily and I go into my room. I get out the book I'm s'posed to read for school and sit in the raggedy old arm chair by the window. Lily sits on my bed, blanket wrapped around her, magazines all over the place. She's singing her Lily song, and patting the pages as if nothing bad ever happened to her, and it's hard to remember it was just a couple hours ago that she was crying into my shoulder.

I must've fallen asleep, maybe 'cause I hate this book. I never nod off when it's science fiction, but this's all about the Civil War. I mean, who cares, it was so long ago and all settled now. They make you learn a lot of dumb stuff in school, but I get done in June, and then I'm outta here for sure, take my truck, go to California or some other place. Maybe live in the desert where's there's no one to bother me. Or get a real job, make some money, live nice. Lots of nice places in California. I'm always changing my mind, except I know whatever I do I won't do it here.

Before I'm all the way awake, I dream like I'm already heading west, driving into the sun. But when I wake up all the way, I'm still here in my room, the house around me quiet. Lily is snugged down into my bed, asleep and breathing thick, not snoring exactly, more like a bunch of long quivery sighs. Go to the bathroom, piss, splash a little water against my face, peek into Rosie's room. Not home, just like she said. I figure I'll move Lily in there where she always sleeps, 'cept when I go to wake Lily, she cries and burrows down so not even her head sticks out of the blankets. "No, no, no," she cries, "no, no, no." I try a couple more times, but she's not cooperating. I never known Lily to act like this, but who the hell knows. May as well leave her sleep, let her have my bed, who cares.

And Rosie's big bed feels good, the sheets are clean and cool against my bare skin. I can see the new moon out the window. Doesn't take long before I'm asleep again. Next thing I know, there's someone in the room with me, shuffling around in the dark. I'm lyin' on my side, facing the window, so I can't see who's there. Rosie maybe, come home after all? But I smell beer and old sweat, I don't know what else, except nobody could smell like this but Pops, must be Pops.

I lie still, trying to keep my breath slow like I'm asleep and thinking he'll go away, but Pops comes over to the bed and slides the covers back from my shoulders and sits so the mattress sags down with a groan. Then he puts his big rough paw against my side and slides it down over my hip, and I sit up wicked fast and swing my feet over the side of the bed and stand between the window and the bed. "What the fuck," I say to him, and I see him swinging his head back and forth like a bear before it charges. "Pops, what the fuck are you doin'?"

He rubs his hands over his face and keeps his head turned away from me, and then he says, "Well, look at this, I guess I got the wrong room," and he stands up and starts backing toward the door, so I turn on the light, and there he is in all his splendor, naked as a jay bird with his hands down over his prick and his head turned away from the lamp like the light hurts his eyes. "Sorry," he says, "didn't mean to bother you," and then he's out in the hall, closing the door between us.

I don't follow him, but I hear him going along the hall and down the stairs, and then a couple minutes later his car starts up. I look out the window, but he's gone already. All's I see is the red taillights going over the crest of that hill down the road. I find my clothes where I dropped them, and I sit on the bed so's I can pull my pants on, but it's like I can't move a single muscle. I just sit there with my clothes in my hands. What the fuck's happening here? Then I get dressed, except for no boots, and go into the hall.

Daisy and Violet have their door shut. I push against it, but it stays still. Locked? That's impossible, but something heavy's stopping that door from opening. Pretty sure they're both in there, why else block the door? I quit pushing, walk to the front of the house and listen outside where Mama and Pops sleep. I think I hear Mama snoring, but I open the door to be sure. Like I figured, Mama's asleep, no sign of Pops.

Now my room. Everything's like I left it, quiet and neat except for the magazines on the floor. Lily is snuggled way down into the blankets. I sit on the edge of the bed. I'm trying to be calm, trying to figure everything out, but I guess Lily feels my weight on the mattress 'cause all at once she's sitting bolt straight up in the bed with her hands raised up in front of her like she's scared I'm gonna grab hold a her. "No, no, no," she says just like before.

"Hey, Lilio, it's me," I tell her. "Hey, Potato Cake," but there's no laugh this time.

So, Sunday morning. No avoiding it I guess. I'm driving my truck, not knowing where to go, but sort of headed west, away from the sun, and Lily's asleep on the seat next to me. She's still in her red dress, but I've found her some shoes and a sweater, and I wrapped the blankets from my bed all around her and grabbed the loaf of bread from the kitchen. When I brought her out to the truck she's like, "Where we going? Where we goin'? We goin' to see the deersies?" so I told her be patient, it's a real long way to the deer place. Lily pulled that folded up picture of the fawn out of her pocket and smoothed it flat against the seat and patted it with her hand, and then she curled into the blankets and slept.

I know pretty soon Mama will wake up and wonder where we are. Rosie will come home and wonder why we went, unless maybe she already knows. Daisy and Violet will move the dresser away from their door and not care if we're home or not. And Pops? Most likely he'll come back, listen to his music, sing a couple arias or whatever with the fat guys, and then tomorrow put on his clean coverall and act like the world's the same as ever.

All that time, Lily and I will be driving someplace, except I haven't figured out yet where, or how we're s'posed to live, or who to tell what has to be told.

Do No Harm

I AM HERE, but they do not know it. They think I am a child. Or a fool. They speak to me in loud, careful voices, using simple words. And I? I do exactly as they order. It is easier that way. I open my mouth for the pills. I extend my arm for the blood pressure cuff. I put on the clothes they bring, and I sit quietly in the chair beside my bed. I am a good girl, they tell me.

But I am not a good girl. I listen to their simple, uneducated voices. I hear them chattering together in the hall after the doctor goes away. They think he is cute. Easy for them to say. They don't have to endure his questions, his prodding fingers, his little experiments. He has a long, narrow face and pale eyes. His teeth are small and sharp, the teeth of a fox. "Ritalin," he said to me yesterday. "We'll try you on that. It'll give you some pep."

"No," I said. "It's poison."

"We've been very successful using it with Parkinson's," he said, and the edge of a threat crept into his voice. "That and electroshock therapy are our two best tools with someone as depressed as you."

"No. Nothing more."

"We'll talk about it tomorrow," he leaned so close to me that I could smell his breath and see the orange hairs growing on his nose.

"No." I turned my face away. He thinks I am his toy, that he can change my mind with one drug or another, that he can make me want to walk up and down the hospital hallway in my paper slippers, make me dress and go downstairs for bingo in the afternoon.

I do not play games like bingo. In all my seventy-eight years, I have never played such games.

Bridge, yes, cribbage, yes. Games of the mind. Because although they do not know it, I do have a mind. It is alive inside my head, curled and silent like a tiny animal, waiting for its chance to flee.

I know this disease. It will steal the power from my arms and legs. It will silence my voice. It will freeze the expressions of my face. The nurses tell me I am doing well. How could they know? They have not watched my slow diminishment. I sit down to write to my brother and see the letters grow smaller as they cross the page. The words shrivel, my hand cannot control them. It is the same with my voice, my thoughts, the connections in my brain. I count the losses as they accrue and know that I am vanishing, obliterated slowly by my disease.

I close my eyes. I hear the rough breathing of the women in the other beds. Maria and Mary. Maria's bed is so close to my chair that I could reach out and touch her. If I wanted to, if I cared to. But I am saving my strength, hoarding it until the time is right, and then I will be gone from this hospital and never again hear the voice or breath or cries of Mary and Maria.

It is Friday, and downstairs they have been cooking fish. I can smell it. Its greasy tentacles touch my face. I can hear the carts out in the hall, the cheerful, vapid aides delivering the lunch trays, urging us to eat and get strong. I will not open my eyes when they come. I will not eat their greasy fish. "Sibyl," one of them is shouting. I hear her pull the little plastic table in front of my chair and set the tray onto it. I hear her snap open the waxy carton of milk. "Sibyl, it's lunch time. Time to wake up." I am silent. She will not stay. Too many other patients wait.

Anne comes each day at noon. She is my niece, my friend,

my goddaughter. Every afternoon she sits by my bed and wills me to be well. Today she is wearing shoes with hard soles. I hear her in the hall, then in the doorway, pausing, watching me while I pretend to sleep. I have known her since the day she was born, and until now—until I fell and had to be carried out of my house on a stretcher, lashed down like a piece of driftwood, carried through the dark yard toward the red flash of the ambulance—until now, she has always done what I asked.

She is beside me, speaking softly, as if my silence smothers her. "Sibyl, it's Anne," she touches my shoulder. "Aunt Sibyl, hi."

I open my eyes and stare at her. She is wearing a red jacket, and tiny diamonds sparkle in her ears. Her hair is gray like mine, but hers is thick and bright, a halo around her face. "My angel of mercy," I say. "Have a seat."

"Sibyl, don't you want your lunch?"

"I want my dogs. I want to go home."

Anne rises, lifts the plate of cold fish and goes. I hear her shoes against the linoleum.

When she comes back, she will want me to eat, she will dip the spoon into the Jell-O and hold it toward my mouth. She loves me, I know, and I think that she will help me if I tell her how.

"Take me out of here," I say to her. I will not let her eyes escape mine. "Take me home. Don't leave here without me."

I see that I terrify her when I am like this. I must wait. I must give her time. "Well," I say, "at least help me get to the bathroom," and I raise my good arm, the one not shattered when I fell. Anne takes my hand and steadies me by the shoulder. "Thank you," I say with formal politeness, and Anne, dear, dull, obedient Anne, follows me to the bathroom and unbuttons my pants for me.

When we come back, the room is full of sound. It is Mary. She has turned on the television and lies flat in her bed, the remote control pressed to her belly. She is watching, or not watching,

Who's Afraid of Virginia Woolf. The volume is high. Elizabeth Taylor screams brutal, drunken insults at Richard Burton. I glance at Maria, but she has turned toward the window and is praying softly in Portuguese—a language the nurses do not even try to comprehend.

I skitter toward my bed. Tiny,rapid Parkinson's steps, dangerously unbalanced. Festination, the doctors call it. Anne follows, afraid I will fall, afraid to interrupt my forward motion. At my chair I stop. "Help me turn around," I order, "then go see, please, if you can find some applesauce."

Anne looks at the TV, at Mary, at Maria, at me, crumpled again into my chair. I see that she is exhausted, dark hollows below her eyes, lines of worry around her lips.

"Sibyl," she says, "isn't there another room we could go to—someplace quieter?"

"No." I am stubborn. I want her to feel the dark and casual cruelty of this place. "I'm not allowed to move from here."

"Of course you are. Let me get the wheelchair. I can push you down to the sitting room, or we can take the elevator and go to the sun porch."

"There's only one place I want to go, and you know where it is." Anne sits on my bed.

Elizabeth Taylor and Richard Burton have another drink. Maria says another prayer. Anne will not stay much longer; she cannot bear such noise. "The applesauce?" I remind her gently, and she goes into the hall to forage in the nurses' kitchen for food that will slip easily down my throat.

Anne. I call her my angel of mercy—a joke, sad because it is true. She has been at my house and seen how I spend my days—balancing the food, the liquids, the Sinemet—medicine I hate but can no longer live without. And here, where I have been put to heal, surely she can see that my caretakers have become my enemies. They want me to eat when I cannot swallow. They want me to sleep when my body is humming. It is their schedule we follow, not mine, and without my own routines I cannot maintain the precarious balance that lets me live.

Anne is back. She has the applesauce. She has a spoon. She sits on the bed and feeds me so slowly and tenderly that I could cry.

"I must get home," I tell her.

"But how would you manage, all alone?"

"There is you," I say. "There is my brother in Boston. There is my neighbor who feeds the dogs and watches the house. There is the community nurse. I can manage."

"But if you fall again?"

"I will use the walker," I promise, pleading with my eyes for her to believe me. I hate the walker, but I will use it. I will push it slowly in front of me everywhere I go. I will no longer hurry in my tiny tiptoe steps round and round inside my house. There is a circle that I travel when I cannot sleep—living room, bedroom, hall, kitchen; living room, bedroom, hall, kitchen. In my circles, I am not alone. My dogs follow, click-clicking behind me through the house. The bathroom is there, just by the hall. The kitchen is there, everything I need, the foods I like, the foods I can swallow, the spoons and forks with fat, soft handles that I can hold and never drop.

"And the nights?" Anne asks.

"Better home than here."

Here, the nights are worst of all, but I do not tell that to Anne. Part of me wants to protect her, save her knowing how my body will not rest, nor my brain. How Maria prays and cries all night. How I dream of flames. I am in the house with my dogs. They howl for me to save them. I see the flames and choke in their smoky heat. But I am in a high bed with metal rails and cannot escape. Every night, I live my death, and when I wake, a nurse—some child, young enough to be my own, the one I never had—tells me it is nothing. "Only a dream," she says.

The fox, my doctor, is back. Anne and I both sense him at the doorway. I curl inward even before he pads into the room. Anne stands, nervous, smoothing her skirt. "Should I go out?" she asks him.

"No, I'll only be a minute." Anne walks across the room, stands at the window by Maria's bed. The fox comes to my chair. He steps close to me, so close and tall his face is hard to see. I have to bend my neck back to watch his mouth.

"The girls down in physical therapy are pleased with your progress." His teeth are very sharp.

"They tell me your insurance will cover another week of therapy." He has slicked back his hair so that the straight tracks of the comb slice through it.

"Then I'll be talking to your brother about where you go from here." His pale eyes slide across me, dismissing me.

"It's my life, not my brother's," I say.

He hears the challenge in my voice and steps back, away from me. He glances toward Anne, but she is staring at the trees outside.

"Your arm is healing well," he says, retreating to a safer subject.

"Then send me home."

"Not yet. Maybe next week. There are tests I need before you go, and a new anti-depressant."

"No more tests. No new medicine." The muscles in my arms are tense and shaking. My hands leap across my lap like rabbits playing in a field.

The fox points to my arms, "Are you upset, Sibyl?"

"No," I say.

"Your arms are shaking. I think you must be upset."

"A little," I admit.

"You're a little upset, Sibyl? Nervous? Do you want to run away, Sibyl?" I can sense Anne motionless by the window, listening to the fox. "Why are you upset, Sibyl?" He uses my name like a whip.

"I can't last in here much longer."

"A couple more days. There's no point moving you somewhere else before your insurance runs out."

"Wait," I say. "Don't leave." I cross my arms against my chest and try to press them into stillness.

"We'll talk about it Monday," and he goes.

I relax my neck, let my head fall forward, close my eyes. Anne walks to my bed and speaks to me, but I do not reply. Suddenly a nurse is here, offering me ginger ale. "I never drink ginger ale," I remind her. "I tell you every day, water—no ice."

"Oh, I forgot, honey." She takes the ginger ale away. I wait for her to come back, knowing she will not.

Finally Anne gets up, leaves the room, returns. I hear her pour the water. "Not too much—only half full," I say, eyes still closed. She holds the cup and puts the straw against my lips. I drink a little, turn away. "You've got to get me out of here."

"He frightens you, doesn't he," Anne whispers, and, although I do not want to, I begin to cry. "I want to be home," I plead. "I want my dogs, my books, my big blue chair. I want the African violets in my kitchen window."

Anne reaches out to smooth my hair, but all she says is, "Oh, Sibyl."

It is Saturday, and I have persuaded Anne to bring the dogs. Just bring them in the car. Let me see them, I have begged. Yes, I have said, I will let you take me in the wheelchair, down in the elevator, outside into the parking lot, whatever you want. On Saturday, routines grow lax. The nurses have different faces. There is no bingo, no physical therapy, no doctors on their cushioned feet, stealthy in the halls. On Saturday, no one is watching.

I am dressed and in my chair. My hair is combed. My cane leans against the bed. The little animal inside my head sits alert and ready as Anne comes up the hall and through the door and touches my hand. Does she feel my bones, thin as a bird's, and see the quiver of my heart?

"I'm ready," I say. "Do you have the dogs?"

"In the car. You can see them from the window."

"Yesterday you said we'd go downstairs." I take the part of the petulant child.

"Okay, we'll go downstairs."

"Yesterday you talked about the wheelchair."

"Okay, I'll find one. You sit right here and wait."

I cannot wait. I find my cane, steady it against the floor, rise and walk slowly to the window. Anne's car is parked carefully in the shade, windows open just enough to give the dogs fresh air, but from here I cannot see the dogs. Then Anne is behind me with the wheelchair. Her hands on my shoulders, she guides me down and back. She lifts my feet and settles them on the footrests.

"You won't need the cane."

"I might," I say and cling to it. Anne hooks it over the back of the wheelchair, and we go out.

The driveway is hot and bright. I squint toward the car and see the moment at which the dogs see me. They bark and beat their feet against the car windows and bounce on the seats, leaping from front to back. Anne stops the wheelchair next to the car. I talk to my dogs, saying their names, praising them, exciting them even more. They spin and pant and drool and wag their long golden tails. I feel strong again, invincible. I turn to Anne. "I want to get in with them."

"They're so excited. I'm afraid they'll hurt you."

"They won't." I press myself upward from the wheelchair. The chair starts to roll back.

Anne is there, stopping it, setting the brake. I take her arm and stand. "Now open the door."

"Sib, they weigh more than you do and they're so excited." We both know that she is helpless against my will.

I lean toward the window, "Down, Dawn. Down, Dusk."

They sit immediately as I knew they would—as I have trained them to do.

"Now," I command Anne, "open the door and help me in."

The dogs watch, obedient and eager. I get into the car and pull my cane in behind me. "Okay," I say. The dogs are all over me, licking my face, my arms, my hands, the three of us whining in joy. This, this is the medicine I need. I beckon Anne closer. "They're thirsty; can you find some water?"

"Are you sure you're okay?"

"I promise." I will promise anything. "Get the water." I watch her walk, retracing the way we came. She glances over her shoulder once, and I wave, cheerful, safe, a good girl. But I am not, have never been, a good girl. The moment Anne disappears, I lean forward to lock the doors of her car—first the back, then the front.

When Anne returns with a bowl of water, I am exactly as she left me, a dog leaning against each shoulder. I watch as Anne reaches for the handle of the back door, squeezes the latch, pulls, frowns. She pulls again, not understanding. Then she tries the front door and knows what I have done. "Sibyl, unlock them!"

"No. Take us home."

"I can't."

"You can and you know it. Take us home."

"What about your clothes? Your medicine?"

"I have everything I need at home. Get in. Drive. It's easy."

"Who will take care of you?"

"Me. I will take care of myself, just as I have always done. Look, I have unlocked the door. Now you can get in."

Anne gets in and sits behind the wheel. She watches me in the rearview mirror. She grips the steering wheel so tightly that her fingers are white. "You're asking too much," she says. "What if something terrible happens? I'll never forgive myself."

"I forgive you everything."

"Sibyl, you can't just quit, you can't give up."

"I won't," I say to her. Not yet. Not now. "This isn't giving up. This is staying alive."

Anne is silent, watching me.

"You've always trusted me," I say.

Reluctantly, Anne reaches forward, turns the key, starts the car. "Oh Sibyl, we are going to be in such trouble when they find out."

"That will be my problem, not yours." I am exhilarated. I have not felt better in years.

The dogs stand up and fan me with their tails and breathe happy clouds against both back windows.

I lean forward to rest my hand on Anne's shoulder. "Now drive, please drive me back where I am me."

Nesting on Empty

JUNE AGAIN, and my birthday. We sit at the dining room table, each of us in the place we have always occupied, David at the head, so tall, somehow steadier than the rest of us. He provides the center of our family, the fixed point around which we revolve. Nate is at David's left. He's twenty-six now with a degree in physics, but settling down doesn't seem to be in his immediate future. After dinner he will drive back to Vermont, where he is a woodworker and plays mandolin in a bluegrass band. Tess sits at David's right, across from Nate, her floppy brown hair, dark eyes and quick, crooked smile mirroring his. Tess will turn thirty in September. She is living with us for the summer, or until she finds a job. "Just a month or so," she reassures me. "I'll be gone before you know it."

I am at the end of the table convenient to kitchen, telephone, and dimmer switches for the dining room lights. Tonight, we don't need the lights because Tess has set out so many candles in low crystal holders. I look across the candles at David and at the children we have raised. They are kind and careful people, generous with their love, confident in their good health. I open the gifts they've brought. A cake of soap from Tess, the kind I like best but never buy because of its cost. From Nate, a bird in flight that he has carved and polished from a curving sweep of tiger maple. David gives me a silk shirt, a beautiful pale shimmer of blue, expensive, and exactly like the one he gave me last year. I lift it from its box for all to admire. I touch the silk to my cheek.

Tess says what a good color, how great with my eyes. Nate, less skilled at lying, says, "Nice, Dad. That's really pretty."

"I thought it looked like you," David tells me. I am careful not to glance at Tess. Sometimes when we get to laughing, we can't stop.

David raises his glass for a toast. He shuts his eyes in concentration. Tess reaches for my hand and holds it hard. "Happy birthday," David says. He hesitates and studies the wineglass as if surprised to discover it in his hand. Then he asks if I will share another sixty years with him.

David is almost seventy, and lately he's having trouble with numbers. We've been married thirty-five years, not sixty, but he's right about the birthday number. I tell him yes, God willing, sixty more years will be just fine. Nate and Tess applaud. Their father has remembered everything he meant to say. Now we can eat.

"I got myself a present, too," I tell them. They look at me, indulgent, mildly curious. "Chickens," I continue. "They're out back right now, in the dog run. Three hens and a rooster." I know this will set the children off, and I wait with pleasure for what they will say.

"No, Mom, please, not chickens again." Nate folds his hands against his face in mock prayer.

Now Tess: "Remember the hen whose feet rotted off?"

Tess knows exactly how I will respond: "Her feet didn't rot," I say. "She burned them when she crossed the hot asphalt on the new driveway. It wasn't her fault."

"Remember the one who fell into the water barrel and drowned?" Nate asks.

"What was the name of that chicken with no feet?" David asks.

I interrupt to tell them that I like chickens. Chickens are interesting. Chickens amuse me. "That was Rhoda," Tess tells her father, "as in 'Rhode Island Red.' She was the partridge in the pear tree in our fourth-grade pageant."

"She was the hit of the show," David remembers. "I think I have pictures of her somewhere. I bet they're in my desk."

"Later, Dad." Tess touches his arm to keep him at the table.

When we are ready for dessert, Nate clears the dinner plates and returns with bowls, spoons, and three pints of ice cream—coffee, chocolate, raspberry swirl. We hand the pints around the table, scooping what we want into our bowls. The bowls are just for show, a flourish of formality in honor of my birthday. More often, we eat directly from the cartons. Tonight we savor the sweet chill of the ice cream and talk about nothing in particular. White wax from the candles drips onto the table. In the kitchen, our old dog, Maggie, rattles the broiler pan that Nate has put on the floor for her to lick. I think of the fragility of life, and I am frightened by our good fortune.

When Maggie was a puppy, David hung sleigh bells on the inside knob of our front door and taught her to ring them when she needed to go out. Maggie is thirteen now, "Ninety-one in dog years," David frequently reminds us, "older even than I." She rings the sleigh bells indiscriminately, but one of us always hurries to open the door for her and waits to hoist her back up the porch steps when she is ready.

Lately, David doesn't notice the bells. "Are you getting deaf?" I ask. He accuses me of mumbling. This has become a predictable exchange. We think little of it, but Tess is alert for signs of our folly or decrepitude. She exudes a thin edge of disapproval when I let Maggie out or help her in, or when Maggie carries her bowl in her mouth and drops it at my feet, a plea for food. When Tess's friends phone, she tells them, laughing, that her father is deaf and her mother is co-dependent with the dog.

"Maggie can't help it," I say. "She's a retriever. Retrievers are bred to carry things."

I have been thinking more than usual about inherited traits

and weaknesses. My maternal grandmother lived to be ninety-two, my father held out to eighty-seven. There's probably hope for me if stay on my guard. I do the crossword in *The New York Times*. I swim at the Y. I take long walks, think good thoughts, eat vegetables and fruit. I practice yoga every morning and go faithfully to my writing workshop once a month. And, for now at least, Tess is here. Simply having her in the house energizes me; I catch myself humming bits of old songs or smiling into the mirror in our front hall.

Even so, there are days when I could happily stay in bed, shades down, phone unplugged, summer blanket lightly over me. Today, a Thursday in July, the sun already pricks at the curtains, but I wait. One lovely minute more before I push back the covers and set my knobby feet onto the floor. I listen for the sounds of our life. Tess is still asleep upstairs, I know, but David is in the kitchen rattling dishes as he unloads the dishwasher, oblivious to Maggie and her insistent bells. From the henhouse in our backyard, I hear the rooster crow for freedom. David no longer hears these sounds that pull me from bed.

When I come into the kitchen, I see that David is wearing his earphones. He is dancing as he carries clean plates and glasses from dishwasher to cupboards. The earphone wire snakes behind him and connects him to the stereo like the umbilical cord of some half-formed animal. I say good morning, but he points to the earphones and shakes his head. In my nightshirt and bare feet, I go outside to free the chickens and watch while they scratch at the ground and chuckle their approval of the cracked corn I throw to them.

When Nate and Tess were in grade school, David and I bought ten acres of wooded land overlooking a wide tidal river. We built this house and have lived here ever since, the river and the salt marsh our only neighbors. Over the course of those years, Nate and Tess grew up and moved away. We too got older—graying hair, a slower walk, series tickets to the symphony, a family membership in the bird club. David plays golf, fishes at the mouth of the river, and has lunch once a week with three men he's known all his life. I am more solitary, happy to stay home. In winter, I write my stories and watch the swans glide up and down the river. In summer, I sail and tend the garden.

Though we're retired now, David and I worked hard for everything we have—he was a lawyer, I a teacher. We cared for our children above all else and put them both through college; we stayed out of debt, though it was hard, especially in the college years. Each of us has recently lost a best friend to cancer. Other friends, some of them younger than David, have sold their homes and moved to condominiums overlooking golf courses. They urge us to follow their example. We are too far out of town, they say, too alone. What if we had to call for help? What if the EMTs couldn't find our house?

But I have planted dogwood and lilacs and hundreds of scilla and daffodil bulbs. David has cut and maintained sinuous trails through the woods. We have put up bluebird houses in our field. The tree house David built for Nate and Tess is still in the big oak. In a series of sad occasions, we have created a graveyard for our pets and planted it with lily of the valley. A small dock at the bottom of the yard is home to our Boston Whaler and a 12-foot cat boat exactly like the one I sailed when I was a teenager.

"It isn't time," I tell our friends. "Not yet."

I have been sailing all afternoon. Because the wind is perfect, the tide high, the August sky a hot, milky blue, I have stayed out longer than I intended. I am alone. I prefer to sail alone. Instead of worrying about my passengers—Do you need sun block? Would you like to take the tiller?—I can enjoy the way my little boat lifts to meet the wind, the slither of water along the hull, the flight of the heron above the marsh.

Ben and Tess disapprove, but I am impatient with their cautions. "I've sailed alone since I was just a kid. You can't expect me to stop now."

This afternoon, when I turn the boat toward home, I see that the sky to the north is piled with thunderheads, their bottoms black with rain. I know the storm will move my way—thunderstorms come up against the wind—but there is plenty of time. I pay out the sheet and let the southwest breeze push my boat ahead of it. Just before I reach our dock, the water goes flat and reflects the black sky. The oaks along the shore hush and hold their breath. In a moment, the wind will come again, fierce and sudden, from the opposite direction. I uncleat the halyard, drop the sail, pull the paddle out from under the deck, and stroke for the dock. By the time I have tied up the boat and furled the sail, the northeast wind is driving the rain against me and the thunder seems close, loud and crazy.

Though I am already soaked, I run exhilarated from dock to house and fling open the back door. Outside, rain beats down, thunder crashes closer. I listen for David, Tess, Maggie, but hear nothing. I let the door slam behind me, go to the laundry room, strip off my wet clothes, and dump them into the washing machine. I hear a sound from the dining room, indistinct, mixed with the rattle of rain against the windows. I hurry into the bedroom, grab the robe from the hook in the bathroom, pull on a dry pair of underpants. My hair lies flat against my skull, darkened by the rain. I am fleetingly surprised how young I look without the gray. I leave the bedroom, turn into the dining room, and hear scuffling sounds from beneath the table.

For half a second, I am almost afraid, but I kneel on the dining room rug and peer under the table. Tess is there, crouched with Maggie beside her. "Hi, Mom," she says.

"What are you doing?"

"Hiding from the thunder. Maggie was upset. We couldn't find you."

"Oh Tess, I was sailing."

"You're not supposed to go out alone."

"It was wonderful."

"Weren't you scared?"

"You should talk. Look at you cowering here."

"It was Maggie's idea."

Maggie leans against Tess's shoulder. Thunder reverberates, so close that the house shakes. Maggie curls her body into a defensive circle. I crawl under the table and put my arms around my daughter and my dog. "Mom, I was worried about you, I knew you were in the boat."

"You can't expect me to just sit around the house and get old."

"Don't say that, Mom."

"I mean it, though. Your dad is getting old. He can't hear me; he has slowed to a crawl in everything he does. I'm getting old, the dog's already old. I've glimpsed the future, and I don't like it."

"I'd go sailing with you any time, you know. You don't have to go alone."

"But you weren't home, and the tide was high."

Already, September is here. Tess has moved to New York City to take a job with the International Rescue Committee—she tells me I should describe it to my friends as a non-governmental humanitarian organization. The house seems wrong without her.

Then Nate phones from Vermont to see if we will take care of Nellie, his three-month-old puppy. She'll be good company for me now that Tess is in New York, he says. And it's just for three or four weeks, while he goes hiking in Utah with his girlfriend and two friends from work, maybe some other people, he isn't sure. Things are slow right now at the woodworking shop, so they're closing down for a while; he's always wanted to spend time in the West; who knows, maybe he'll decide to move there for a few years. "So can you take her, Mom? Please?"

Nate brings Nellie the next weekend. He also brings all of

her equipment and a list of what he calls her vocabulary words. He has written them out carefully for me so I will not forget: Sit, Come, Go peepee, Down, Drop that dead mole. He explains her routine: three meals a day at precise times, no sleeping on the bed, no scraps from the table, no chewing on anything except the dog toys he has brought.

As I listen to this list of rules, I realize how clearly Nate perceives my weakness as a disciplinarian. Maggie sleeps on our bed. She licks our breakfast, lunch and dinner dishes before I put them in the dishwasher. She will work for hours to get burned food off the inside of casseroles or pans. She rides in the passenger seat of my car and pants a milky layer of dog slime onto the window.

"No problem," I tell Nate. "But send postcards if you're ever near a mailbox."

I try my best with Nellie. I keep her off our bed at night. I do not feed her table scraps. But I do encourage her to lie beside me on the couch so that I can embrace her puppy warmth, and I designate an old pair of David's slippers as legal dog toys. David doesn't notice, and Nate, I hope, will forgive my lapses as easily as I forgive his.

In October, not long after Nellie's arrival, my favorite hen vanishes. I search everywhere but cannot find Dottie or even a telltale scatter of her white feathers. I decide she has been eaten by the fox or the red-tailed hawk, or possibly by Nellie, and I abandon my search.

"Well," I say to David, "hawks get hungry, too, I guess."

"What?"

"Never mind."

A few weeks later, I find Dottie and seven babies, tiny as thistle down, scratching among the late blooming asters. She has been hiding somewhere, sitting on her eggs. She has chosen a perilous time of year for hatchlings, and so I try to catch them. They are small but very quick, too quick for me. I wait for dark, watching out the kitchen window to see where Dottie will lead them.

Nesting on Empty

"What on earth are you doing?" David asks.

"Waiting for the chickens to bed down so I can catch them." David shakes his head and pours himself a scotch. I know he has not understood, but it doesn't matter.

Just before dusk, Dottie leads her brood under our front porch. I give them time to settle, then go outside with a flashlight and a cardboard box. Dottie hears me coming and chatters a warning, but she is helpless in the dark. I grab her with both hands, hold her wings against her body, lower her into the box and close the flaps over her. Then the babies, easy to catch, but I worry about crushing their fragile bones.

David and the dogs are waiting for me in the kitchen. "What's that?" David asks.

Nellie jumps against me and sniffs at the box. "Down," I tell her. "Baby chicks," I tell David. I find Nellie's leash and clip it onto her collar and hand the loop to David. "Hold her for a minute, please."

I drag Nellie's training crate from dining room to kitchen, empty it, and line it with *The New York Times*. David drinks his scotch and watches me slide the box of chickens into the crate and tip out Dottie and her brood. "Here you go, babies," I say. "Welcome home." Dottie cackles loud protest, collects her chicks, tucks them under her, and stares defiantly at me from the far corner of the crate.

David asks, "How long?"

"If I leave them outside they'll surely freeze."

"Surely," he says and, still holding Nellie's leash, wanders off to watch TV. Maggie picks up her bowl and follows me around the kitchen.

Because I have given not a single thought to making dinner, David and I lock Nellie and Maggie in the garage and drive to our only neighborhood restaurant. We sit side by side in a booth so that we can hear each other, and we order wine, salad, and bowls of thick red vegetable soup. I watch as David spoons his soup carefully into his mouth. I feel strange, as if my head is somewhere else, as if my husband and I are miles apart. I lean my shoulder lightly against David's, interrupting his careful lift and dip of soup. "How many people in here, do you think, have eight chickens living in their kitchen?" I ask.

He puts down his spoon and looks at me, startled. "None, I guess," he laughs, dribbling soup from spoon to shirt.

I have driven to Cambridge for my writing workshop at the home of a retired professor. My fellow writers are women, some as old as I, some closer to Tess's age. I tell David this mix of ages and perceptions is good. "Very interesting," I say. "Stimulating," but I wonder if that's wishful thinking. The younger women write about love and sex and alcoholic parents. The older women write romantic fiction, family chronicles, or memoirs of youthful exploits.

Today we discuss Mindy's story. I have read the story twice and made careful notes in its margins. In two years of workshop, Mindy has written again and again about the birth of her first and only child. She is angry—outraged, actually—because no one warned her of the pain, the mess, the worry of parenthood. As the other women comment on Mindy's work, I am silent. I can think of nothing good to add, and I wonder how Mindy will deal with life's more permanent betrayals.

I know the length and frequency of Mindy's contractions. "The timing of the contractions—such an effective way to build tension in your story," Anne murmurs.

I know that Mindy's water broke while she was selecting cantaloupes at Bread & Circus. "I love the way you use the cantaloupe as a symbol of ripeness," Margaret says.

"Write what you know," encourages the professor. "Use strong verbs, let us share your sensations," but what do I know? I feel the world slip past, so gray and silent you wouldn't even see it go unless you were watching for it.

When the discussion ends, I hand my written comments

across the table to Mindy. I murmur about my husband's dinner, the weather, the traffic. I say goodbye, find my car, take the parking ticket off the windshield, and drive out of Cambridge in a slow, raw November rain.

Traffic is terrible. By the time I get home, the sun is down. No lights have been turned on in our house, but David's car is in the garage. Could he be asleep? I walk toward the house and am almost at the porch when David speaks, "You're finally here." He sits on the top step, waiting, apparently, for my return. I see his face as a pale blob in the darkness. His shoes scrape on the wooden steps as he stands up.

"David, what are you doing?"

"The roof keeps the rain away," he reassures me.

"But why are you out here?"

"The doors are locked."

He must be wrong. We never lock the doors unless we plan to be away for an entire day. I step around him and try the latch. Inside, Maggie pokes her nose against the sleigh bells, eager to join us in the rain. David is right. The door is locked.

"See?" he says.

"Did you try the back?"

"Of course, do you think I'm stupid?"

"I have a back door key. You stay here; I'll go in through the kitchen."

"Okay." He is strangely obedient.

In the kitchen, Maggie greets me and leads me to the front hall. As soon as I open the door, she bolts out past David and squats in the garden. How long has she been locked in and David out?

David comes, walking stiffly, into the house. "You must be freezing," I say. I guide him to a chair near the fireplace. "Let me get a fire going." I am busy with the paper and the kindling, but I am watching David too. He sits motionless, occasionally smoothing the palms of his hands over his face as if he is wiping cobwebs from his eyes.

I bring him a drink, some cheese and crackers, his warm

green sweater. I take the other chair by the fireplace and wait for David's explanation. When it doesn't come, I ask, "Who locked the doors and why?"

"We never lock the doors," he tells me. "Never need to."

It is January, Christmas and New Year's Eve safely behind us. David and I are at Logan Airport, worried and sad. Tess is with us, scared and excited. She's going to Sierra Leone for six months, sent there by her employer to oversee one of their humanitarian aid programs. When she got the job with IRC, I failed to imagine—or chose not to imagine—that she would need to travel, to live on her own in some country that, until last week, I couldn't find on a map. Now I am full of questions. Where will you live? What will you eat? Who else will be there? What about AIDS? What about malaria? Tess is tired of my fears. She doesn't know the answers either, she says, there's no point asking.

She has been home for the weekend to pack and say goodbye. Nate and Nellie drove down on Saturday to see her, and the three of them went for a long walk on the wintry beach. A sad walk, I think. Tess cried when Nate said goodbye to her. Because I did not want to cry, I left them embracing in the driveway, while David stood to one side and rubbed Nellie's ears.

Tonight Tess flies from Boston to Amsterdam, then to Sierra Leone. I do not ask about the kind of plane or how many changes she will have to make or where she will land or how she will get from there to wherever she is supposed to go. David doesn't ask either. He has told me again and again that she will be fine, that she is young and healthy and careful.

Six months isn't all that long, he says.

Maybe so, but a week ago—we knew then about Tess's job; she was due home on Friday, two more days—I woke around 3 A.M. and did not hear David breathing next to me. I reached for him, found the covers thrown back, the sheets on his side of the bed cold. In the bathroom maybe? But the bathroom door was open, the light off. I got up and prowled the dark house. Maggie lay by the front door, and thumped her tail at me. I found a flashlight and went out.

"Where's David, Maggie? Go find David!" Maggie led me around the house and toward the river. I saw David standing on the marsh regarding the stars. When I called to him, he did not reply, and when Maggie went up to him, he stepped away from her and raised his hands to protect himself. "It's just Maggie," I said and touched his arm.

He turned and looked at me. "Oh, it's you," he said.

"Yes, and it's three A.M." I reached for his hand, linked my warm fingers with his cold ones, and led him back to the house.

"I was looking for Tessie," he said. "She was calling me."

"It was just a dream." His words frightened me. "She's still in New York. She'll be here Friday."

Airport security is tight; David and I will not be allowed into the international departures lounge. We stand with Tess in a long line at the ticket counter. We edge forward, pushing her suitcase in front of us. I do not want to be here, I have never liked airports, and tonight is especially bad because Tess is leaving us.

"You could go, I'll be okay," she says, but David and I both shake our heads. We stay so close that we are touching her.

When she has checked her bag, we delay a little longer. "How about a Coke," David asks. "Or coffee?" Tess and I say yes, and watch as David goes in search of Dunkin' Donuts.

"I don't really want any coffee. I feel like I'm about to throw up," she says.

"I know, but Dad's looking for a way to postpone your going through that gate." We watch David at the counter, fumbling for money, balancing three coffee cups, looking for us among the other travelers.

Tess waves to him, both arms above her head like flying.

He grins at her and comes slowly toward us. Tess leans her head against my shoulder. "Dad looks so old. I worry that six months is a long time for him.

"I hope he'll be okay." She steps back from me. "I hope you'll be okay."

David and I find our way out of the terminal. The air is cold, bitter with the smell of jet fuel. A great weight grows inside my chest, a ragged chunk of icy granite. David walks beside me past the rows of cars. There is nothing to say.

When we see our car, I start toward it, but David catches hold of my arm. I turn half to him, questioning. He wraps both arms around me and pulls me hard against him and will not let me go. "What are you doing?" I ask.

"I'm holding on," he answers. "I'm holding on for dear life."

We cling to each other in the parking lot. The mercury vapor lights hum like insects, and plane after plane rises at an impossible angle into the sky and roars away. A man stops his car near us and honks impatiently. He signals that he wants our parking space.